FLOWER O' THE BROOM

When Dinah Heywood offered to work for Dr. Sandie, who ran a summer school in St. Pierre-de-Lys, she found that although his students adored him he seemed prejediced towards her, and Dinah thought him unsympathetic, particularly towards a good-looking young man they gave a lift to on the last lap of their journey. And it was this young man she was to meet again . . .

JANET BEATON

FLOWER O' THE BROOM

Complete and Unabridged

LINFORD
Leicester

First published in Great Britain in 1981 by
Robert Hale Limited
London

First Linford Edition
published May 1991
by arrangement with
Robert Hale Limited, London

British Library CIP Data

Beaton, Janet
    Flower o' the broom. — Large print ed. —
Linford romance library
I. Title
823.914 [F]

ISBN 0–7089–7042–7

Published by
F. A. Thorpe (Publishing) Ltd.
Anstey, Leicestershire
Set by Words & Graphics Ltd.
Anstey, Leicestershire
Printed and bound in Great Britain by
T. J. Press (Padstow) Ltd., Padstow, Cornwall

1

"JUST imagine," I said, "if it had been like this yesterday!"

My mother and I standing at the lounge window stared at the streaming rain, at the puddles collecting on baked earth, at the roses that had been a glory of colour, drooping now under a weight of water. We had been hard at it, all morning, she and I, packing away glasses and plates and cups, ready to return to the caterer's next day, while my father had been lugging furniture into its normal position from where it had been set for the buffet reception.

She let out a long breath. "I just wish I knew that Julie and David had arrived safely!"

"You're a proper old fusser!" I squeezed her shoulder. "They aren't going to ring up from Corfu. Anyway, honeymooners don't ring people. Other people don't exist!"

She leant her weight against me. "Dinah, I'd never have got through yesterday without you!"

"I just did what any sister-bridesmaid would do! You were a smashing bride's mum!"

"Everybody said it was a perfect wedding!"

"The sun shining, the garden looking like something in a glossy mag, all the pretty dresses and the hats and the *food* — Of course it was a perfect wedding!"

Only it hadn't been for me. Not one hundred per cent perfect. David Parr had been my find, and to my dismay, after all these months, I had been conscious of jealousy, contemptible and irrational jealousy.

I said, "Dad's gone to ground with the Sunday papers. Shall I make us some coffee?"

"That would be lovely." She flopped into the chintzy chair. Her hair-do had lost a little of its chic. She wore no make-up and looked ten years older than she had looked the day before, receiving her guests on the terrace with the wisteria in soft blue drifts behind her.

In the kitchen I boiled up milk. David Parr! Perhaps it was because our meeting had been so dramatic that I had been sure David was *it*. I would never forget as long as I lived driving up the motorway no distance out of Bexton, seeing a little red car take the corner on the other carriageway just too fast, the wheels touch the far verge, to come on in a kind of fascinating slow motion, swinging round, going over on its roof, bouncing, clearing the central reserve, settling a few yards in front of me, side-on, absurdly sedate and four-square on its wheels.

People have told me since that the first thing to do is to wave down the on-coming traffic in case there is a pile-up, but I didn't think of that. Other people did. I dashed for the red car, wrenching open the door, afraid of what I should find. And there was a woman squatting

3

up on top of the driving seat, amidst a jumble of parcels and luggage, with the back window out and on the road behind a scatter of newly dug potatoes and a bottle of wine intact!

I was with her on the roadside when the ambulance arrived and in the ambulance was the young doctor, tall and lean and efficient. Afterwards he had dropped by to let me know that, incredibly, the woman was none the worse and to make sure I wasn't suffering after-effects of shock. Or so he said. After that he came often. He was in casualty in the big local hospital and sometimes he was so tired he could hardly keep awake.

I am a passionate romantic. I saw my life mapped out before me. In supporting him, I would serve humanity. And then my sister Julie, two years younger than me, training in London to be a physiotherapist, came home for the weekend. The fairy godmother who dispenses gifts was in a generous mood when Julie was born. Her hair is fairer than mine, almost ash-blonde, her skin magnolia-pale, her eyes large and blue fringed with lashes that are long and black. And most important of all, she has a sweet gentle nature, the capacity totally to care and to trust. I couldn't blame David for falling in love with Julie. She was right for him as I wouldn't have been. I had seen all that quite clearly. I had got over the hurt or so I had believed until yesterday when, standing behind them in the mellow old church, I listened to the centuries-old words of pledging troth and felt alone and on the outside . . .

I carried the coffee into the lounge. My mother was just a moment too slow in straightening from where she had been hunched over the arm of her chair, her head in her hands.

"Mum! Planes *do* land safely! And Julie and David will be very happy!"

She smiled brightly. "I know!"

I handed her a cup. "What's wrong, then?"

She produced a puzzled look that was almost convincing.

"H'm?"

"Have a biscuit. I don't imagine *you* ate much yesterday. Now, what's worrying you?" And then I guessed. My elder sister Melanie, who hadn't come to the wedding. I sat down on the rug beside her chair. "Don't feel too bad that Melanie didn't make it. But it would have been quite a tackling getting herself here from the South of France. Jasper is only four, after all, and a bit of a handful — "

"That isn't why she didn't come."

"Melanie is quite broad-minded, Mum! She wouldn't feel Julie was letting the side down having a white wedding in church, doing everything properly!"

My mother's chin came up. "What Melanie has done with her life isn't something to be facetious about, Dinah!"

"No. But it isn't something to blow up out of all proportion the way you and Dad do, and make into a Greek tragedy. Okay, she went off with a painter and lived with him, but they got married eventually — "

"She was only eighteen. She didn't know what she was doing. But Daniel

6

was old enough to know. And they didn't get married until just before Jasper was born. I wonder why they bothered!"

"Oh, Mum! I hate to hear you all bitter!"

She put her hand on my head, twisting a strand of my hair. "I'm not bitter, just sad for her. And your father has hated it all so much. He has high principles himself. He thought the world of Melanie. His first-born daughter! For a man that's something very special. It broke his heart seeing her go off like that."

"But you can understand it. She was his student at art college. He was larger than life. He had charisma!"

"If only she had come home to England when Daniel left her! Your father was so hurt when she wouldn't."

"She had her pride, Mum. And then she was making a real go of the shop by then. I beg pardon! The *atelier!* You couldn't blame her for choosing to stay in St Pierre-de-Lys. After all, she was a painter herself when she had the time.

She has that romantic old house — "

"Romantic to visit in the summer! But can you imagine what it would be like to run, with the atelier to manage and a child to look after!"

"Anyway, she has coped marvellously. And now there's the glamorous Raoul Chenier dancing attendance, wanting to make her his own, if he hasn't already — "

"Dinah!"

"Oh, Mum, don't be so stuffy! Melanie and her sort don't live their lives quite as we do. Let's not pretend! Anyway, now that her divorce will soon be through, the glamorous Raoul is pressing her to marry him so that he can carry her off honourably to his posh villa on the Riviera. So what's the problem?"

My mother drew in a terse breath. "She's broken with Raoul."

"What?"

"I rang her up a couple of weeks ago to find out just when she would be arriving and if Raoul was going to be able to come to the wedding with her. She was quite casual about it. 'Raoul?' she said. 'Oh, that's off!' I didn't handle it well on the phone. I was so taken aback. Your father and I liked Raoul when we visited her last summer. We felt so thankful that she had met someone like him, involved in the art world too, with his gallery in Antibes, who could give her a lovely home and security after all the mess — I said all the wrong things. I hurt her, the last thing I wanted to do. But you know how she can be — flying off the handle on the instant. 'We live in different worlds,' she said, 'and we'll just have to accept the fact! As far as Julie's wedding is concerned, you'd better count me out!'"

"Oh, darling! And I suppose Dad blew his top!"

"I haven't told him. I just said Melanie couldn't get away after all."

I stared up at her. "You've been bottling all this up?"

"I've been so busy it wasn't so bad. But now — "

"Yes, I can see."

"I'm just so worried about her. She has lots of friends out there, I know. But they're a butterfly lot. I'm scared she'll do something silly — like before!"

"Well, Mum, you know what you've got to do."

"What?"

"Get yourself out to St Pierre-de-Lys."

She sagged in her chair. "Don't think I haven't considered that. But I can't."

"Why not? I'll look after the old man, see that he gets his bacon grilled in the morning and his slippers toasted when he comes home!"

"He has more than enough on his plate right now. We've had the wedding — he has been on the stretch about that. And there's the merger going through in the office which means a double workload and a number of functions that I'll have to attend with him. If Melanie were ill or in dire need I'd have to go. As it is, I'm putting your father and his well-being first. He has worried about Melanie over the years, suffered over her

10

nonsense — Nobody knows how much he suffered. But Melanie is twenty-eight years old. She has chosen how she wants to live her life. It's not what we would have chosen for her. Parents have to let go. Your father has done all he could. I'll let him find out about Raoul gradually. For now he deserves peace."

"But *you* aren't going to have any peace."

My mother was twisting that strand of hair until it was beginning to hurt.

I said, "For your own sake, maybe more than for hers, I think you must go and see her. Inside, she's a very serious person. It could be she is really very lonely. Daniel and she used to be so close. He was very *real*. We adored him, you know, Julie and I — "

"You were children that one time we stayed with them."

"Not so much children. I was seventeen. He could have ignored me or talked down to me or teased the way so many men do tease girls at that stage. But he was charming — "

"Oh, he could charm! But you need more than charm in a husband — "

"Go out to St Pierre-de-Lys, Mum!"

My mother got to her feet. "No, Dinah."

I stood up with her. "I'd go like a shot if I had any leave. But I've just had this week off for the wedding, and then there was that walking holiday in the Lakes with the crowd — "

When Julie and David had announced their engagement and it had been important to get away with my own friends. "Not that Melanie would talk to me the way she could have talked to you. But I could have found out quite a lot — And just by going I'd be showing we still cared. Perhaps I could have persuaded her to come over for a visit. She hasn't ever been back to England, has she? Now, if I could have gone out to St Pierre-de-Lys and kept the shop, she could — "

"That imagination of yours, Dinah, is taking wings! You haven't got leave. Let's see about lunch."

Next morning I had no great enthusiasm for going back to the office. Everything felt drab and flat after the excitements of the wedding. The rain had stopped but the sky was leaden. Water swished from my tyres as I freewheeled down the hill into Bexton. The narrow streets of the town were congested with traffic and jay-walking pedestrians. I was thankful to reach the peace of the Old Quadrangle which housed the administrative offices of the university where I was on the secretarial staff. The modern university with its lecture theatres, laboratories and refectories had long outgrown its mediaeval nucleus and had spread among lawns and trees a mile or two out of town.

The students had been down for weeks and on the noticeboards sad posters flapped proclaiming forgotten discos and dramas alongside faded lists of names in degree exam results. The only notices that were fresh and relative to life that was still to be lived were those advertising courses at the Summer School at St

Pierre-de-Lys. It was no coincidence that I was seeing them now. They had been up for a week or two and the name had registered with me every time I passed them. St Pierre-de-Lys Provence, a beautiful old town with an annual Festival of Music and the Arts, where my sister Melanie had a little art gallery. Only this morning for the first time I stopped and read the poster. The Summer School was run by the Extra-Mural Department of the university and included courses in French language and literature, history and architecture, geology, flora and fauna of the area . . .

There would be opportunities to visit the art exhibitions and concerts organised by the Festival. Demand for places was heavy and early application was advised. I couldn't get myself on a course, could I? On unpaid leave, perhaps, to improve my qualifications? It might just be worth inquiring.

I had assumed that the Extra-Mural Department would have its offices in the Old Quad. When after some asking around I discovered that they were housed in the same block as the Extra-Mural lecture-rooms and library out on the campus my enthusiasm cooled somewhat. Nevertheless, any way of getting to St Pierre-de-Lys that summer was worth investigating and when lunchtime came I un-padlocked my bicycle from the rack and set out.

In the Extra-Mural Department the woman I saw was enormously enthusiastic.

"Wonderful, those Summer Courses!" she said. "We have people queuing up every year for places."

"So I haven't much chance?"

She smiled as one does to a well-intentioned nitwit. "Of getting a place *this* summer? If you put your name down now you might just be lucky for next year! But do have a copy of the prospectus!"

Parking my bike outside the staff club, I collected something to eat in the snack-bar. As I ate I flipped through the pages of the prospectus. There was an aerial photograph of St Pierre-de-Lys, the modern city spreading out from the old hilltop town. I remembered it quite well from the couple of visits I had paid Melanie, that first time when the exotic Daniel was around, and then after he had decided the chains of matrimony weren't for him and he had taken off to fulfil his genius in unshackled freedom.

From the next table a birdlike little woman smiled. "Going to the Summer School?"

Her grey-haired companion gave an elaborate sigh. "Dear Dr Sandie!"

The birdlike woman said, "We went on a course the year before last. Not to study the language. We didn't want that. More to learn about life in France. We stayed in a wonderful old rambling place with flowers! I can see it still. Two weeks we had. I don't think I ever spent a happier holiday. Those fascinating lectures and expeditions — "

Her companion said, "You get fantastic value. It's Dr Sandie, of course. Nothing was too much trouble for him. If there

16

was anything you had a notion to see he'd fix it for you. If you wanted a book he'd root it out. It's just too bad," she went on, "about Dr Sandie's Millie!"

"Dr Sandie's Millie?" The birdlike woman wasn't so well informed.

"She's going into hospital to have an operation. It will break her heart to miss the Summer School — "

The two women talked on about Dr Sandie's Millie. She was his secretary and as marvellous at her job as he was at his, it seemed.

I set down my coffee cup. "What happens," I asked, "about a replacement for Dr Sandie's secretary?"

The grey-haired woman eyed me.

"I'm in the Social Sciences Department, secretarial. But we're very quiet at the moment and I wondered — "

"Go along and see Dr Sandie! He will have to find somebody."

Back in the office I gave the suggestion some thought. There was so little doing that there was plenty of time to think. It might be worth a try! At the end of the afternoon I got on to my bicycle and retraced my route to the Department of Extra-Mural Studies.

The enthusiast at Enquiries was just packing up.

"Dr Sandie?" She smiled broadly in answer to my question. "Oh, *he's* around. Never leaves until after everybody else! You'll find him at the end of the corridor, the door straight ahead."

I walked along the passage. The sky was still grey, with rain drizzling and the light was dim. I wished I could have tidied up a bit. My hair that I wear just short of my shoulders, flicked back and with a fringe, had been really pretty at the wedding. Now damp air had flattened it so that it hung lank and heavy. The print dress that had been crisp that morning flopped about my knees and its lime colour clashed with the strident orange of the waterproof anorak I had had to put on for the rain.

I drew a long breath as I reached the door at the end of the corridor.

Everybody spoke well of this Dr Sandie. He wouldn't eat me. There was no need to be nervous. The worst that could happen was that he would say No. I knocked.

A voice called, "Come in!"

After the corridor the room seemed large and light, with great windows giving on to grass and trees. Shelves lined the walls with a chaos of books and files and papers. In front of me by a littered desk stood a man. He was younger than I had expected, thirtyish, with thick, dark hair, straight, thick eyebrows and a marked five o'clock shadow on upper lip and jowl. He was wearing an inelegant roll-top sweater and was chewing on a pen.

He looked at me from dark eyes as I came in, closing the door behind me. "Yes?"

"Dr Sandie?"

He took the pen from his mouth and frowned at it as though he had just detected a peculiar taste. "You wanted to see me?"

"Yes, please. If it's not inconvenient."

"You aren't in this year's classes and if it's next year's courses you want to discuss it might have been more helpful if you had made an appointment or come in office hours. However, since you are here — " He jerked his pen towards a chair.

I sat down. "It's not about a class. I'm a secretary in the Faculty of Social Sciences. I heard today that your secretary is to be unable to go out on the Summer School and I wanted to ask — "

"If you could take her place!" He lowered himself into a swivel chair. "What an efficient grapevine we have! Could the Faculty of Social Sciences get by without you?"

I thought of my mother and Melanie and remained in the cold plastic chair. I even managed a smile to show that I recognised sarcasm when I met it.

"I think they just might!"

He smiled too, but it wasn't in any kindly way. "I imagine they would."

I said quickly, "I speak French

reasonably well. I've been to France quite often — "

"And you like it?"

"Oh, yes! It's lovely in St Pierre-de-Lys — "

"You know St Pierre-de-Lys?"

Too late I knew I had made a mistake. "I have spent holidays there, yes."

"And you'd like another, paid!"

"It isn't like that!"

"And no doubt there are people in St Pierre-de-Lys you'd like to see again!" He got briskly to his feet. "I'm sorry. I have my own methods of engaging staff — "

"Before I came to the university office I worked in a travel agent's. I have experience of — "

"*Thank you!* I am grateful to you for offering to help out."

I got to my feet. I knew when I was beaten. He picked up his pen and flicked the ballpoint in and out.

"Close the door as you go," he said. "And it might be as well if you read what's on it!"

I let myself out. It was darker than ever in the passage after the light in his room. I shut the door and bent to the name-plate. "Director of Extra-Mural Studies in French Language and Literature. Dr Jonathan Alexander."

I stared at it in dismay. Sandie, an affectionate pet name for Alexander! It must be his nickname among all those adoring students who got such good value from his marvellous classes! My cheeks burned with shame. As I pedalled away I had to face into rain and I was glad of it.

At home I spent a miserable evening. Later, I knew I'd be able to laugh at my encounter with Dr Sandie but right now I felt snubbed and silly.

I helped my mother cut and box up wedding cake. She chatted away, about weddings in the past when she had been a bridesmaid. She had been pretty — she was pretty still — and popular too, so that she had been a bridesmaid quite often.

"I got quite worried," she declared,

"wondering if I'd ever be a bride!"

"As if *you* had to worry!" I said.

There was a box to be addressed to Melanie, a much larger box than the usual size, with a chunk of cake for Melanie to cut up, and some icing titbits for Jasper.

"Mum," I said, "won't you explain to Dad and go to St Pierre-de-Lys?"

"I wrote Melanie a long letter straight after our disastrous talk on the phone. I asked her to write back. Her present came for Julie, but not a word for me. No Dinah. It's no use."

The next few days dragged. A card arrived from Corfu, smudged with sun-oil, with crosses for kisses. My father was busier than usual. My mother was tired and edgy and determined not to let it show. I became edgy too, obsessed with a feeling of uselessness.

The rain cleared and the sun came out. A fresh crop of roses blossomed in the garden. I felt more out of step with life than ever. There wasn't enough happening in the office to keep me fully occupied. When one morning Mrs Woodford, our austere boss in the Social Sciences Secretarial Department, called me over to meet a Miss Bowden who had dropped in I wondered why I had been singled out for the chat that followed. She was plump and easy in her manner, with untidy greying hair and bright eyes that twinkled a lot. Without appearing to do so, she asked about my work and I realised what she was after was attitude and motivation. I did not care to ask around who this Miss Bowden was. Could it be that I was giving less than satisfaction?

I was taken completely by surprise when, a couple of days later, Mrs Woodford said, "Report to Miss Bowden, would you? In Extra-Mural."

Extra-Mural!

Mrs Woodford was on the telephone and I had no chance to ask her anything.

At the Extra-Mural Department the enthusiast at Enquiries took me along to Miss Bowden's room. It was next to the room I had visited before. This morning in bright sunshine the place seemed all glass and light. Miss Bowden welcomed me with a cup of coffee. "I suppose you know why you're here," she said.

"Not exactly."

"I understood you were interested in standing in for me on the Summer School?" So Miss Bowden was Dr Sandie's Millie!

"I did offer, but — "

"I have to go into hospital, you see. I've been waiting for months to have this wretched op. and it has to come along now — "

"I'm sorry."

"Oh, I'll be glad to get it over with. But I didn't want to let Dr Alexander down. I offered to postpone the op. so that I could do the Summer School as usual, but he wouldn't *hear* of it. He knows I'm finding things a bit heavy and that I'd have to go back to the end of the waiting-list at the hospital. 'Just find me someone to take your place!' he said. 'I leave it entirely to you!' There was somebody I had in mind, but she can't leave the country at the moment. A friend told me about meeting you in the Staff Club. She didn't know your name but when she said you were with Mrs Woodford it was easy. She is a special friend of mine and I got a glowing recommendation from her on your efficiency and conscientiousness, and your ability to get on with people, which is as important as anything. Frankly, I was looking for someone of my own age. Then when we met I thought, 'How nice to have somebody young and pretty for a change!'"

The sunshine through the plate-glass was strong where I sat in a linen skirt and jacket, but I felt chilled. There were some embarrassing moments ahead unless I said, *Miss Bowden, I'm terribly sorry, but I've changed my mind!*

I had opened my mouth to speak the saving words but she was already on her feet with the door open, saying briskly, "Come along and meet Dr Alexander. After that I'll make a start to showing you what your job's going to be."

Miserably I followed her out and

waited while she knocked on his door and pushed it open. The typed name on the card blazed at me as if it were in neon light.

"Dr Alexander," I heard her say, "here is your new secretary for the Summer School, Miss Dinah Heywood!"

She swept me forward. He straightened from fighting with a drawer in his desk. His thick hair had fallen forward over his straight brows which suddenly came down to a V and his dark eyes were positively stormy.

"What?" he said, thrusting back his hair and turning the dark eyes on her. Miss Bowden would have gone through the unwelcome introductions all over again.

"I understood — " he began and then he broke off, turning abruptly to the window. "Thank you, Miss Bowden. If you would excuse us — "

Miss Bowden snatched some files from the desk and took herself off.

He turned then and didn't try to pretend how he felt.

"I want an honest answer," he said. "You've been politicking for this job, haven't you?"

Being angry is a good stiffener. Until now I had wanted simply to get out of that room. "I am not in the habit," I said crisply, "of giving answers that aren't honest. I have not politicked for the job, as you put it. I wouldn't know how to set about it! Miss Bowden came to see me the other day. I didn't know she was from Extra-Mural. If you want to know why she picked me, you had better ask her! Shall I tell her you want to see her on my way out?"

He reddened and I waited for the explosion.

Suddenly I was rather enjoying myself. I didn't care very much now what he said. His students might think he was the greatest thing since sliced bread. Obviously he created an image for them and was proud of it. But I felt that in being regarded as unworthy to be his secretary I was having a lucky escape and doubted if I wanted to go to St

Pierre-de-Lys quite badly enough to endure working for this egoist!

"I should like to see Miss Bowden, yes," he said quietly. "And will you please wait."

From Miss Bowden's room I could hear nothing. The sun streamed in on her plants. Who would care for them while she was in hospital? Her walls were hung with posters. The gargoyles leered on the roof of Notre-Dame de Paris. Shade dappled the water of the river that ran beneath the arches of the Pont du Gard. A glorious sunset reddened mountains behind the Riviera. It would have been good to go to France. I loved it. I could understand Melanie's unwillingness to leave it. In the sunshine I could almost sense the compound smell redolent of wine and garlic and Gauloise cigarettes-

The door opened. A rather flustered Miss Bowden came in, leaning back against the door when she had closed it.

I said, "I'm sorry, Miss Bowden — "

"He's in a mood, this morning. Not like him! Raging about things not back from the printers that they've had only a few days! Be an angel and type up this schedule for me and then we can get down to what this job will entail!"

"But I thought — "

Already she was thumbing through folders, selecting papers. "And take a carbon!" she added. Had he said nothing to her about me?

I was bewildered then and remained bewildered until I had had time to sort things out. Apparently, after all, I had the job. Dr Jonathan Alexander did not want me for his secretary. He wanted Miss Millie Bowden. She understood his work. She knew his ways. But he couldn't have Miss Bowden. Any substitute she produced he would accept, in spite of reservations and doubts. Only towards me there were greater reservations and doubts than there might have been to some. Meanwhile, Miss Bowden had to drill me for the Summer School job. Another member of the Extra-Mural staff would take over her normal work as Dr Alexander's secretary.

It was a little time before I felt sufficiently confident to break the news to my mother. She laid down her knitting.

"Going to St Pierre-de-Lys with the university? *How*?"

I gave her an edited account of what had happened.

"And so I'll be able to see lots of Melanie over these four weeks. She can't put up any sort of front for as long as that!"

My father, too preoccupied with the office merger to notice my mother's low spirits, didn't suspect as anything more than coincidence my going to St Pierre-de-Lys.

"You can tell Melanie we were very disappointed that she missed the wedding," he said. "And you will meet Raoul."

The days flashed by. Miss Bowden went over my duties thoroughly, and soon I was handling all paperwork connected with the Summer School.

"You'll do," she said. "You'll do very well! Dr Alexander really is in luck!"

I knew Dr Alexander didn't think so, however. Always he was polite, scrupulously careful to make sure that I understood what was required of me. But there was a cold formality in his manner that should have eased, and didn't, something almost of distrust.

He had explained at the start how the students some coming for one week, others for two or even longer, flew out on arranged charter flights or made their own way to St Pierre-de-Lys. "Miss Bowden always travelled with me by car," he said, "and it would be as well if you would do the same. There are always last-minute arrangements to plan and discuss. We go quite fast with an overnight in Paris with friends of mine."

And so it was that one glorious August morning I set off in the passenger seat of Dr Alexander's car en route for France. My suitcase in the boot contained an exciting range of dresses, separates and sunwear that I'd picked up in the big stores. The briefcase on the back seat was stuffed with papers and I had attained the dignity of a clipboard. My feelings were mixed. For my mother's sake I was deeply thankful that I would soon be in St Pierre-de-Lys with the opportunity of seeing Melanie over several weeks. A letter had come at last from Melanie, acknowledging the wedding cake, with a lot of frothy chit-chat pointedly omitting any reference to her personal life and problems. Contact was to be maintained apparently, but on a purely surface level and my mother's anxiety had deepened.

From the moment of setting out, Dr Alexander had made it clear that he didn't want small talk when driving. I had hoped that, arrived on foreign soil, he would close ranks, as it were, but France was probably so much a second home to him that he felt no need of it. I offered to map-read him in Paris as I had done for my father but he said, "Thanks, no. I'm fine."

Apparently he knew the one-way street system in Paris as well as he had known it in London. Feeling superfluous and increasingly nervous about meeting his friends I sat tense in my seat while he coolly negotiated the fast-moving traffic in what seemed countless lanes.

In a quiet street shadowed by plane-trees he drew up at a handsome block of flats. The professor with whom we were to stay was a few years older than Dr Alexander, tall, balding and very tanned. Madame Romain was what the French call *une jolie laide*. Her mouth was too wide, her teeth too prominent, her nose high-bridged and angular, but she had a kind of polish, style, glamour. Beside her I felt very young, very much a little girl from a quiet country town. They both spoke English well and out of kindness to me did so as long as they remembered.

It was the first time I had seen Dr Alexander in a social situation, and it was something of a revelation. Like his students, Professor and Madame Romain seemed to adore him. The professor kissed him on both cheeks, Madame hugged him and planted kisses on his dark face as though she meant them. He chatted cheerfully, half in French, half in English, there were private jokes and references to friends in common and shared experiences. Apparently they had all known one another for years.

As soon as I decently could after an excellent dinner I excused myself on the pretext of being tired. It was true enough and I felt they would want to be on their own. Madame Romain took me to my room. It was ridiculously large for me, with great windows swathed in misty net.

"You will be comfortable, yes?" She threw open the door leading to a beautifully appointed bathroom. "Usually it is Miss Bowden who comes with Jon. She is so good to him. She looks after him so well — "

Oh, *yes,* I thought wearily. *Your adored Jon is having it rough this year! But he'll survive!*

"Miss Bowden is — what do you say — the clucking hen! It is much better for him with you, young and pretty. Only perhaps — "

Taken by surprise I stared at her and she smiled. Then more to herself than to me she spoke some words in French and shrugged "*Eh bien!* Sleep well! Tomorrow you have to be up with — *l'hirondelle, n'est-ce pas!*"

I giggled in a rush of affection for her.

"That's swallow, isn't it? You mean the lark!"

"The lark! But of course. What is it your poet says,

'Hail to thee, blithe spirit,
Bird thou never wert — '

Good dreams, *chèrie! A demain!*"

I was in bed, half asleep when suddenly my subconscious, having done its work like a good computer, put what she had said into my mind, all efficiently processed into English . . . ' . . . if only your hair had been black, your eyes like midnight . . . ' So there had been someone in Dr Alexander's past, young and pretty and dark! French probably. And she hadn't taken kindly to his overbearing ways! Drowsily I thought I couldn't blame her, Dr Sandie's Dark Lady . . .

We left Paris very early next morning and took the Autoroute to the south. From the number of yawns he gave in the first hour on the road I gathered he and his friends had sat up talking late. He drew in at an Autostop sooner than I expected and took his coffee black. He had passed a great pile of typed sheets over to me as we left the Paris flat, passages in French, presumably for translation, or study, and I had to insert them in my files with the material relevant to a series of lectures. From time to time he would ask me to make note of some items on a memo pad.

On the Autoroute one feels cut off from the real life of the country, bypassing towns. I glimpsed great forests, widely spreading fields where already the corn had been harvested. The sky was blue with constantly churning clouds. As the day wore on it grew very hot. The clouds were no longer white but massing in towers grey and blue-black. It was no surprise when a thunder storm broke.

Dr Alexander cut his speed. Time was wearing on. When he left the autoroute he seemed relieved that I took up the road-map from the shelf and checked the route. Rain was coming down steadily from a lowering sky, obliterating the countryside, flooding the road. The busy windscreen-wipers barely coped with the driving water. We had expected to reach St Pierre-de-Lys in daylight, but already it was getting dark. The route-finding was difficult here. St Pierre-de-Lys is six or seven miles inland from the coast and a wrong turning could have taken us into the busy built-up area along the Riviera. There was a map-reading light in the car and with its help, keeping my fingers crossed, I read the route through one small town after another, peering in the light of the headlamps through the rain for confirming road-signs.

There came a bad moment when I was sure I had made a wrong decision. For some time now he had been relying on me. He was tired, worried that we were arriving late, concentrating wholly on the actual driving. When I saw a sign *St Pierre-de-Lys 12km* I gave a cry of relief.

"I was so afraid we were heading for Antibes," I said.

"And you weren't going to break the news to me!" He laughed. It was from relief, of course, from being practically at journey's end, but I felt somehow that he was including me. We were at last beginning to be a team. And then in the headlights I saw the man.

"Look out!" I screamed.

Dr Alexander braked fast and swerved. "What the hell's he doing there?"

"Thumbing a lift," I said.

We lurched past a hooded figure bent forward into the rain. "You can't leave him. Not in this!"

"Can't I? He damn' near caused us to

go into the ditch!"

"We haven't seen a house for ages. It's miles yet to St Pierre-de-Lys. You've *got* to stop!"

With a sickening jolt he drew up on the verge. "All right," he said. "Do your Girl Guide act and see what thanks you get. You'd better remove these papers from the back seat. We don't want to present our students with a mass of sodden pulp."

His precious students! Couldn't he ever forget his Image? I leaned over and cleared the back seat, unlocking the door for the hitch-hiker to scramble in. He wasn't wearing an anorak, but had been holding a linen jacket over his head for protection from the rain, which had plastered his hair flat and was dripping from his nose and chin.

Dr Alexander said sharply in French, "Where are you heading?"

The young man stared dully at us. I said, "You aren't English, are you?" He frowned, running his hands through his hair.

Dr Alexander turned back to the wheel, switching off the interior light. "Tight," he muttered, "or on drugs. What d'you expect from somebody staggering around here miles from anywhere in the dark? St Pierre-de-Lys!" he called over his shoulder. "I'll set you down there. That do you?"

The young man was struggling awkwardly into his sodden jacket. "St Pierre-de-Lys," he mumbled. "St Pierre-de-Lys!"

The name came out slurred. Miserably I had to concede that Dr Alexander was probably right. I had the uncomfortable feeling that quite often he would prove to be right, and infallibility isn't an endearing quality.

From time to time I glanced round at our passenger. It was as well that I had moved the papers and books, for water seemed to have poured from him in floods. He lay slumped in the back, his eyes half closed. He must have fallen in his tipsy progress along the road for one side of his face was grazed, with tiny points of blood among a smudge of mud and grains of gravel. It was a good-looking face, strong-featured, with a finely shaped nose and a clean line of chin. His hair when it dried would be the colour of ripe corn. Suddenly while I watched him he opened his eyes wide.

"Thank you," he said, speaking very carefully. "Thank you very much."

We were in St Pierre-de-Lys before I realised it. There were lights, brilliantly reflected in the wet road, cars streaming past. people hurrying under umbrellas past sparkling shop windows. I recognised a square in the new town where Dr Alexander was drawing up.

"Here you are, then," he said tersely to our passenger. "St Pierre-de-Lys. Out you get!"

The young man's reaction was surprisingly swift. He had the car door open on the instant and with a supple movement I hadn't looked for he was out on the pavement. Once more, very carefully, he said, "Thank you very much." Then the door was shut and he was lost in the dark.

"What happens to him now?" I said.

Dr Alexander had already started up the engine. "That's not our worry. We're here to do a job of work, or had you forgotten?"

No, I decided. Not human!

2

MY memories of our arrival at the Summer School's quarters in St Pierre-de-Lys are a chaotic jumble. From the dark wet night I was pitched into a bewildering warren of a place, with stone-flagged passages, tightly twisting stairs. There were a number of people, most of them French. My ears humming with tyre noise, I couldn't understand what they said to me and somehow I couldn't frame what I wanted to say in French. I remember a meal in a long room, low-ceilinged, with matting in squares on a worn stone floor. I was glad of delicious soup and crisp French bread, but after that I didn't want to eat more. The wine flowed generously, making me pleasantly relaxed, longing only for bed.

Afterwards there was a session with Dr Alexander and my clipboard. I have no memory now of what we discussed; probably I wasn't very clear in my mind then. I remember him gathering up papers and thrusting them into his briefcase, saying abruptly, "That will have to do for now! You're more than half asleep!" and picturing Miss Bowden brisk and efficient, smiling and scribbling down all his instructions. I remember I wasn't unduly worried. After all, I was young and pretty . . .

It was in the morning when I woke up in a tiny cell of a room under the roof, with the sun streaming in from a cloudless sky that I felt worried. I leapt out of bed and got myself downstairs in no time, clipboard in hand, with my hair well brushed, in a neat businesslike cotton dress.

Miss Bowden had briefed me well. I understood the job I had to do. But it wasn't easy at first. The building where I had a little office sandwiched between classrooms had been a monastic establishment in mediaeval times, when the architect had a love of cloistered walks and passages and an eye for a fine vista, but no conception of convenient planning. I found myself walking miles, corkscrewing up and down winding stairs, in the west wing when I should have been in the north. I had known the number of students to be on the courses, but somehow I hadn't visualised them appearing so many. In modern university buildings people fan out. And here, too, the students were older and bulkier and more assertive and also friendlier. I veered between longing for the offhand blade-slim kids in jeans that I was used to and regretting the lack of personal involvement that one normally had in the student life.

La Closerie des Genêts, as it was called, was a college of further education in term-time and had sleeping accommodation for only the tutorial and domestic staff. Our students were farmed out in pensions and hotels all over St Pierre-de-Lys. Lunch was taken in La Closerie, however, a self-service affair in the refectory where we had eaten that first night. Staff ate at a table apart from the students. There was no pecking order and I took care only to be as far from Dr Alexander as I could.

He was busy from morning to night with his teaching and administrative duties. I saw quite a lot of him between times. He was brisk and rather to my surprise not impatient in the early days when I was fumbling a bit. He even smiled once in a conspiratorial way, after he had dealt to their mutual satisfaction with a wiry red-haired little man who wanted to take classes in advanced French language and classes in ecclesiastical architecture which, unfortunately, were conducted at the same hour on the same days.

In my relief at his smiling, I laughed and brought down on my head what I thought of afterwards as his sermon.

"Now, this is just where you have to watch it!" he said. We were in the room where he took his classes on French literature. The ceiling was high, in age darkened wood with carvings where the panels intersected. The walls were of dressed stone with niches where once figures of the saints might have stood. Through the small-paned windows with curving iron bars the sun was glinting on the delicate pink flowers of oleanders.

He was frowning, all formal in a dark shirt with a matching tie. "These courses matter! Think of the people we've got here right now! Older folks like that red-haired bloke who missed out in education, people who are enthusiastic about their subject and spend their summer holiday studying, youngsters filling blanks for qualifications they need. It's serious, it's for real! They've paid a lot of money for their courses. They deserve value! It's our job to see that they get it!"

I hadn't expected a visit to the town in the first few days, certainly not to be able to call on Melanie. At last, however, I felt that I had my job under control. Classes were organised, everything seemed to be running smoothly. Members of staff, most of them French, were friendly, but being neither tutorial nor domestic, I had a kind of freedom that would suit me very well. The time came when I decided I would slip out after classes were over for the day, have a snack somewhere and go to the *atelier.*

For the first time since I had come I put on a frivolous dress. It had very little in the way of straps and a diaphanous skirt in a myriad of pastel colours. I chose sandals with low heels, for I planned to do some walking. I had scarcely been out of La Closerie des Genêts. In the courtyard I looked about me in delight. The walls were of rough stone under a red pantiled roof, the upper floor windows fitted with blue shutters. Wrought-iron balconies under the windows gave it the look of an opera set. Arches on ground level were festooned with bougainvillaea. Geraniums flowered in great earthenware jars, roses bloomed in a tangle, from which dark conifers rose like spears, and exotic palms.

A voice behind me said, "It's Miss Heywood, isn't it?"

I turned to face a tall, angular woman, one of our most elderly students. Lovely blue eyes smiled in her bright face. She was over-thin, with a look of brittle bones and she leant on a walking-stick.

"Hello, Mrs Benson." Just in time I had remembered her name. "It's lovely here, isn't it? I've scarcely seen it until now!"

"You poor girl, you've been so busy getting us organised! We all think you have done a wonderful job."

She was clutching what seemed to be an advertisement for a concert and when I glanced at it she held it out.

"Les Aimants de la Musique Ancienne," I read.

She said, "It's just what I love and it's tonight. The trouble is the friend I was planning to go with is unwell and I'm not sure where it is to be held."

"A l'Eglise Collegiale." It was a year or two since I had been in St Pierre-de-Lys. She wasn't so fit that I could risk making a mistake. "As I remember, the Collegiate church isn't so far up in the old town.

50

It's a *zone piétonne,* but they allow taxis. You'd have to order one, though — right now." I got out my office key. "Would you like me to do that?"

"No, my dear. I enjoy walking, as long as I don't have to hurry. Now, where exactly is this *église collegiale?*"

"There's a map," I began, and then I said, "If you don't mind company, I'll walk with you."

She flushed with pleasure. "But I can't let you do that. You're meeting friends, I'm sure — I'd hold you back."

"No. I was just going to wander around." And Melanie's *atelier* was no distance from the collegiate church.

Conversation was impossible while we were in the modern town, on its crowded pavements, with the ceaseless traffic rushing by. Once inside the old walls, however, we could walk on the breast of the road.

"What course are you taking?" I asked her.

"French literature. I came last year and enjoyed it so much and I learned so much that I just *had* to come again. Dr Alexander has such a fine mind and he has the gift of making complex subjects utterly fascinating."

Another devotée. I smiled.

"Only last year," she said, "I couldn't get about at all. I had just got a broken ankle out of plaster and had to spend my free time sitting in the gardens. This year, being able to explore — "

The road swung out here on the rising contour of the hilltop town and I stopped by the crenellated wall. "If you don't need a breather, Mrs Benson, I do!"

She sat down beside me on the warm stone. "It's beautiful."

The sun was a glowing disk not far above the shaded mass of the hills. The sky was flushed from orange through the palest green to a delicate mauve.

"No wonder they all came here," she said, "the painters to try to catch this light on canvas."

We resumed our walk, in streets that had narrowed and were sometimes stepped. On either hand, tall houses rose within the constricting bounds of the walls. There were a few cafés, some shops sold expensive jewellery, many had prints of pictures for sale. We reached a point where two narrow streets forked. An elaborate fountain threw up thin spirals of water, while pigeons strutted in the falling spray and geraniums and vines trailed over the worn stone.

I said, "The Collegiate Church is this way."

A few yards in the other direction was Melanie's *atelier.* When I had seen Mrs Benson safely to her concert I would slip back. What sort of reception would I get, I wondered. How should I find Melanie, now that I was grown up? Before, she had been for me all vested in the glamour of romance, of love with an artist in an idyllic attic!

The Collegiate Church, handsome in golden coloured stone, stood in a paved square with little shops all round. There was a notice prominently displayed, announcing that doors would open at half past seven and that the concert would begin at eight.

I looked at my watch. "You've just got time for something to eat."

"I won't bother. I'd get all fussed up in case I might be late. The French take so long over food. They look on it as an art form, after all. Trying to rush them is sacrilege."

I laughed. "You're right! But there's a little self-service place in the square — "

"Self-service is so difficult with this stick — "

"Come on," I said. "I'll carry the tray. I'm famishing!"

We had a pleasant little meal. Outside, darkness fell and the lights came on. I was aware of Mrs Benson beginning to fidget and look at her watch, and as soon as we had eaten I led her out of the café. The doors of the church had not opened on time and a mêlée of people surged round the polished steps. Beside me Mrs Benson hung back nervously.

When the doors opened at last there was a general rush. I said, "Keep behind me if you can, but don't worry. I'll get the tickets." For, of course, I should have to stay with her. She wouldn't be sufficiently forceful to get a good seat in the church. And afterwards she would have to get herself down those narrow-stepped streets, lit with beautifully ornate but inadequate lamps. She would be on edge with anxiety all the time, too tense to enjoy the music she so much wanted to hear. I got two tickets and drew her through the milling crowd into the church. "If you don't mind, I'm coming too!" I found her a seat at the aisle where she could stretch out her leg. "I shouldn't have known about this, you know, and it's beautiful!"

The roof and the far corners of the church were in darkness. Light fell on the altar with its sparkling silver and on a smooth floor area of black and white marble. Behind the altar an apse went into blackness. Christ on His Cross rose up into shadow. A harpsichord stood on the tiled floor and two chairs were set with music stands.

I looked at the programme, which

Mrs Benson was studying with obvious pleasure. "Suites," I read, "by Couperin" — that was a name I recognised — "Philidor, Dieupart — " I was in unknown territory. Well, it never did harm to try something new. The details about the players were in French. Their names meant nothing to me and my eye barely skimmed the page.

Promptly at eight o'clock the players came in from a side door beside the altar, two women and a man. The woman who sat down at the harpsichord was older than the others, in a long-skirted dress with overtones of an earlier century. The flautist was pretty, looking one hundred per cent contemporary. Farthest from where we were, a young man sat down with an instrument that at first glance I took for a cello. He was well built, in dark pants and a high-necked garment that wasn't a shirt and wasn't a jacket. The dark outfit highlighted the fairness of his hair and then I almost gasped aloud. It was our hitch-hiker!

Fascinated, I stared at him. Or was

it? He was bending over his instrument so that I couldn't see his face. I became aware that the harpsichordist was talking, in French, explaining the programme. I doubt whether I should have known what she was saying if she had been talking in English. He was tuning his instrument, the good-looking young man with the hair the colour of ripe corn. It was gleaming now in the light from above him. The light touched his well shaped forehead, the strong nose, the thrusting line of his chin. He looked up and exchanged a smile with the harpsichordist, his eyes wrinkling at the corners, a crease deepening in his cheek. There was no doubt about it. He was the young man Dr Alexander had reluctantly rescued from the rain.

I didn't hear much of the first item. The light for reading wasn't very good, the programme print was in an arty style and it took me a little time to decipher that the player of the viola da gamba was called Henri Deloraine, that he had studied in Paris, that he had given many recitals in France and overseas.

The first suite was followed by another. From the programme notes I saw that each was made up of a series of dance forms, Allemande, Sarabande, Gavotte, Gigue, Menuet . . . The harpsichord provided a sprightly rhythmic base, above which the flute warbled gloriously, the viola da gamba providing a rich, darkly coloured tone with a kind of dragging undertow of sound. It wasn't the sort of music I would have stayed with if I had tuned into it on the radio, but I found that as I listened I enjoyed it more and more. At the end of the first half of the concert there was enthusiastic applause from the audience while the players trooped out by their little side door.

Mrs Benson was enthusiastic especially about the flautist.

"That girl is quite well known. She plays in an orchestra in America. Then she got keen on the baroque flute and is becoming more involved in groups like this, giving recitals of eighteenth-century

music with authentic instruments — ”
She had a lot to say about the technical
brilliance of the harpsichordist but didn't
mention Henri Deloraine and I didn't
ask.

The second half of the programme
seemed lighter and more attractive. Maybe
it was that I was adjusting to a new sound.
At the end, as the applause went on and
the players bowed, went out, and came
back to bow again, we had to move
out into the aisle to let people pass. I
moved forward, clapping and smiling,
half hoping to catch the eye of the young
man. He was grinning now, his generous
mouth wide with an attractive line to
his full lower lip. Turning towards the
harpsichordist, he and the flautist paid
their own tribute and as he did so I saw
what could have been a shadow on his
cheek but wasn't. It was a graze, very
faint, above the jawline where that night
I had seen tiny points of blood among
the smeared mud and grit.

Normally I should never have made
a move to attract his attention, but the

atmosphere was warm and friendly and excited. We *had* met, after all! Still clapping as everyone else was doing I gave him the direct kind of smile a friend would give.

His response embarrassed me acutely. Politely he smiled back, but he obviously had no idea who I was. And how could he have had? It was dark that night in the car, and he had been rather the worse for wear. I felt myself blushing, and, feeling rather cheap, I bit my lip and turned away. The players were leaving their marble stage, the audience beginning to make for the door. I got a hand firmly under Mrs Benson's elbow and did my best to make suitable replies to her enthusiastic comments.

It was some time before we were out of the church. We had been sitting well forward and Mrs Benson shrank from the crush at the door. Outside, a couple of young men waited with a van ready to pack up *Les Aimants de la Musique Ancienne.* The outside air struck warm, fragrant with flower and herb smells. I edged Mrs Benson round the van, trying to avoid the cobbles at the side of the church and came face to face with the player of the viola da gamba. Embarrassed enough already, I bent my head to pass but he stopped, saying something in French.

I looked up at him. "I'm sorry?"

He said, "You're *English?* So that's how — "

"How what?"

"Back there in church I got the impression you must have met me, but I'm afraid I don't know you. I mean, it's very much my loss — "

Irritated, I said, "It wasn't in England that I met you. We gave you a lift the other night. It was raining and very dark. You probably didn't see me — "

"What!" His tone and manner changed abruptly. "You gave me a lift back to St Pierre-de-Lys?"

"My boss did. We dropped you off in the square."

"Look, I just can't talk now. But I've got to see you. I *must!* It's vital." He snatched my programme from my hand and scribbled something quickly. "That's my name, where to find me. But where can I contact you, just in case — "

He hesitated and I finished for him " — in case I don't bother? It's all right. I'll co-operate if it matters so much. I'm at La Closerie des Genêts. The name is Heywood."

"Heywood." He nodded, gazing at me searchingly. "I'll ring you tomorrow if you don't ring me. Okay? Thanks a lot!"

He flashed his smile then, with that attractive lower lip sweeping up to the crease in his cheek. Mrs Benson, who had been carried forward with the crowd and had now found her way back to me, was included in the flashing smile and then he was off. He moved fast. I had noticed that before.

Mrs Benson let out a long breath. "My dear, you *know* him,, the young man playing the viola da gamba?"

I could hardly tell her the circumstances. It wouldn't do to touch her evening with even a breath of disillusion.

"I'd met him before," I said lightly. "Now, let's find our way down, shall we?"

St Pierre-de-Lys by night was pure magic, the old stone subtly touched by soft lighting, shops ablaze, lively crowds moving up and down the narrow streets. Conversation reverberated between the high walls, bursts of music came from houses and restaurants. There could be no question of calling on Melanie and I was vexed about that. At the same time I had enjoyed the outing with Mrs Benson and was quite frankly intrigued at my encounter with our hitchhiking yob transformed into elegant musician. Surreptitiously I glanced at his scribble on my programme. But it wasn't the name I had expected. 'Crispin Lingard,' I read with a telephone number and an address in St Pierre-de-Lys.

Mrs Benson was flagging pretty badly by the time we were through the massive gate in the mediaeval walls and out into the modern town, and I was thankful when we reached La Closerie des Genêts. I was quite unprepared to find the courtyard crowded with our students sitting at the little metal tables, downing drinks; the chatter almost as deafening as it had been up in the old town. Just inside the arched wrought-iron gate sat Dr Alexander with one or two of the staff.

He got to his feet the moment he saw us. "Mrs Benson! We were wondering when you'd show up. Somebody, told me you had been hoping to go to a concert — "

"And I did," said Mrs Benson, "thanks to your Miss Heywood. I happened to meet this dear girl and she walked me up to the church, got me something to eat, came with me to the concert. I could never have managed on my own. There was such a scramble for tickets and then for decent seats. It wasn't a very well organised affair, Dr Alexander, but the music — "

"Good, was it?" He was smiling down at her, the night breeze lifting his hair so that in the light of bulbs slung among the acacia trees, he looked young, almost boyish.

"*Good?* That's what I'd call an entirely inadequate word — " She broke off. "Excuse me, won't you? I've just seen my friend. She must be feeling better! Miss Heywood," she turned to me with her lovely smile. "I haven't said thank-you yet, but I shall! After I've had a word with Miss Tweedie there — "

She limped off and I made to follow.

Dr Alexander said, "You must be tired. Let me get you a drink." He pulled out the little metal chair he had been sitting on. The others who had been at the table with him had disappeared. I was thoroughly glad to slump down in his seat.

"I'd love a lager," I said, "Would that be heresy in France?"

"Total heresy! " He grinned, more boyish than ever. A few minutes later he was back with two brimming glasses. Sitting down opposite me, he stretched out his long legs. In light slacks and an open-necked shirt, for the first time he had a holiday look about him.

"It was good of you to take care of Mrs Benson," he said. "That's just the kind of thing I really mind about, as I think you know! If she had come to me about the concert I'd have found somebody to get her there, for she's not all that fit. But she's independent as they come and convinced that we are overworked! You enjoyed the concert too?"

"Very much." I had put the programme in my bag for safe keeping and it was from memory that I reeled off the names of the composers whose works I had been hearing that evening for the first time. I was about to go on and astound him with Crispin when he said, "I didn't know you were interested in baroque music?"

Annoyance stung me through the mellow wellbeing. For all he knew I could be a serious student of baroque music. Why should he assume I wasn't? Any more than he ought to have assumed that Crispin Lingard was a scrounging yob not worth stopping for on a wet night. I shrugged ever so slightly, as though to indicate there was much about me he couldn't possibly guess at.

"Do you play?" he asked.

I sipped the lager, delicious in my dry mouth. "Piano," which could mean to Wigmore Hall standard as well as what it did mean in my case, that I had endured a few years' lessons in my childhood.

He sighed. "I envy you, Dinah. I love music, listening that is. And, I hope, hearing too — "

Just what he was saying barely reached my consciousness. Without seeming to notice, he had called me by my Christian name!

"There are any number of concerts and recitals here during the Festival. You mustn't miss out on what you want to hear. Perhaps you would care to come with me one evening?"

I don't know what I should have said. I was so completely taken by surprise that my mind wasn't functioning very well. A hand fell on my shoulder and I glanced up to find Mrs Benson smiling down on me.

"No, don't get up!" she protested to Dr Alexander, but of course he was already on his feet, helping her into a chair.

"A drink? I'd love one. Lemonade? Oh dear me, no! What are you having? Beer — that's much more like it!" She let out a great sigh and leant back in her seat. "It's been such a perfectly wonderful evening! I've been telling my friend just what she missed up there. And, Dr Alexander, do you know." She fixed her blue eyes on him as he made to go for her drink. "There was such a charming young man standing in for the player of the viola da gamba, who was indisposed. He did very well, considering, with a real feeling for the music. And he's a friend of our Miss Heywood!"

"I don't *know* him," I began, but Mrs Benson was rattling on, giving Dr Alexander a commentary on the performance that could come only from someone who did know about baroque music. Dr Alexander appeared to be listening to her intently, but I knew he wasn't. I had caught the look he had thrown me. That day in Bexton when I had thrust myself forward seeking the job in St Pierre-de-Lys he had taunted me with having friends in the town that I wanted to see. And he believed he was finding his suspicions confirmed. And at what a moment! Just when, for the first time, he had made a movement of friendship towards me. I must put things straight. I had to stem Mrs Benson's happy flow. But fate was unkind. One of the French assistants came rushing up to say he was wanted on the telephone and he went, calling to the Frenchman to see to Mrs Benson's drink.

I waited on but he didn't come back. Then I went up to my little room under the roof. There was a young moon in the luminous sky, and here and there the pinprick of a star. I felt wretched, which was ridiculous. I should be able to explain in the morning. And why should I care what he thought of me? As long as I did my job efficiently why did it matter if he did believe I had sought the job in order to meet up with a friend in St Pierre-de-Lys?

3

NEXT morning I was certain Crispin Lingard would turn up at La Closerie or ring, insisting he must speak to me at an inconvenient moment. When midday came without his having made a nuisance of himself, I thought the least I could do was to ring the number he had given me.

An Englishwoman answered. The next moment he was on the line.

"Bless you!" he said and I could visualise him as he spoke, the quick smile, the creasing of his cheek and the wide curl of that full underlip.

"Mr Lingard," I said, "I doubt if I can be of any help to you — "

"Let me be the judge of that," he said. "The name's Crispin, remember? Let me hear you say it!"

People were milling round the notice-board beside the coinbox phone, which

I had felt in honour bound to use.

"Awkward, is it? Okay! Later, then! Now, *when?* I'd rather it was in daylight and not a minute later than you can manage."

I said, "I close my office here at five — "

"Great! I've checked how to find La Closerie. I'll be at the front gate!"

A succession of small crises kept me busy all afternoon. It was hot. When five o'clock came I would have given much to slip upstairs and shower and join staff and students in the shade of the acacia trees in the courtyard. But for ten minutes a car had been standing by the gate of La Closerie, glossy yellow, low-slung and opulent, and I had a feeling that when I went out I should find Crispin Lingard at the wheel.

I was right, and half the college, including Dr Alexander, saw me walk through the wrought-iron gate and up to the car, the door of which opened for me. I had encountered Dr Alexander on a number of occasions during the day but always when other people were around. I had longed for a chance to explain who my musical friend was, at the same time resenting the ridiculous feeling of guilt he aroused in me. For, after all, there *was* Melanie!

In a white sweatshirt Crispin Lingard looked different yet again from the other times I had seen him. He had the windows wound down for air but even so his tanned skin shone from the heat.

He said, "This is good of you."

I agreed heartily, sticky and weary as I felt.

"I suggest a nice long drink first," he said, putting the car into a vacant space under plane trees. "There's a café here."

I sank into a seat, dappled with deep shade and gratefully accepted a glass of chilled fresh lemon. He sat down alongside me. Pigeons strutted about on the shady walk. Nearby, a flower stall had some bunches left from morning, roses and dahlias and sweet-william, the heat intensifying their mingling smell.

"Let me hear you say it, then!"

I stared at him. "Say what?"

He was smiling, a shaft of sunlight through the plane trees highlighting the fine arch of his nose and burnishing his hair. The lemon drink was sharp and icy. I giggled. "Crispin!"

"Makes you think, doesn't it, of noble knights and troubadours and lovely ladies playing lutes!"

It hadn't, frankly, but I didn't want to disappoint him. After all, he had to live with it.

"That instrument you were playing last night — I don't know anything about baroque music. What was it?"

"The viola da gamba? Ah, sixteenth-century, I think. Reminds you a bit of the cello, maybe? Only it doesn't have a spike to fix it with. You have to grip it with your legs — hence the name gamba, *la jambe* in French — "

"I hadn't thought of that!"

"And you hold the bow differently, sort of inside out."

"Yes, I noticed."

"I started the cello when I was a kid — had no choice with one brother a fiddler, another playing the clarinet, with a sister for the piano! I got interested in the old instruments a year or two back. It's quite a rage these days, playing early stuff with contemporary instruments — "

"You mean that instrument was as old as *that*?"

"Oh, no! A few might be, but most are careful imitations."

"I hadn't realised you were English or that you were standing in — "

He laughed. "Then you really can't know much about it! The other two are professionals. They were really stuck last night and so they bore with me."

I said, "So you aren't really a musician? What do you do for a living then?"

"In computers, maybe? Not so romantic!"

"I dislike computers. The things they do to people's salaries and gas bills — "

"Ah, well, let's not start on that!" He glanced at his watch. "I can't go on calling you Miss Heywood, and time is passing."

"Dinah."

He savoured it on his tongue, looking at me appraisingly. "Yes, Dinah is fine for you — blue eyes, good nose, wide mouth, all that fair hair — Cheeky, just a little. And sweet underneath and sensitive. Loyal — "

"Why don't you set up as a fortune-teller? That's the kind of thing people cross your palm with silver to hear!"

"When I'm broke I'll try it! Now, Dinah — " Suddenly he was all serious. "Tell me what happened the night you picked me up."

All the light patter had been leading up to this. "It was dark," I said, "raining hard."

"Did I say anything?"

"Just 'Thank you very much'." Carefully, but I couldn't very well tell him that.

"And I toddled away quite happily when you dropped me off?"

"I couldn't see you — not once you'd left the car."

"You thought I was drunk, I take it?

76

And that the cool rain would sober me up? It didn't occur to you that I could have had an accident?"

"Oh, *no!*"

His glance was bitter. Crispin Lingard could look quite formidable. "Mildly concussed. I came to later on in the hands of the *gendarmerie,* who had formed the same opinion as you. They delivered me back to my address when I was able to tell them what it was and next morning very kindly drove me out to where I told them I had ditched the car. Everything beforehand was crystal clear. Only what happened after, until I came round in the cells, has gone. And that's where you come in."

"Crispin, I'm really sorry — "

"What I want you to do is help me if you can to find out exactly where I was when you stopped to give me a lift. I've no idea, you see, how long I had walked or how far. I don't even know what direction I was walking in. If I take you to where I left the car will you try to carry on from there." Already he was on his feet.

I said, "I'll try."

The traffic was heavy as we left the town on the road northwards, and I didn't want to worry him with questions.

"I could have been lying on the verge, for all I remember," he said.

"You were trudging along with your head down into the rain. I think you glanced back when you heard the car. I'd have said you thumbed a lift."

"The old student tricks coming back! It's a bit disturbing, you know, when there are a few hours of your life missing!"

"You had your jacket over your head."

"Ah! That's how I could have lost her!"

"What?"

He smiled wryly. "Actually, it's a wallet I'm looking for."

From the valley floor with its discreet industrial estate among oleanders and acacia trees we rose on the farther hillside into a luxury world of sumptuous villas tiered in flourishing gardens to the crest. Geraniums flowered scarlet in jars, in great tubs, in solid-packed beds. There were carnations in profusion with their heady scent, roses, exotic cactus and palm trees. All day the sky had been pearl-coloured in heat. Now blue was showing mistily as if through fine gauze.

Over the crest of the hill we were in different country, running first between plane trees with the sun spattering light on their dappled trunks. The road was rising again and the plane trees gave way to oak. Already the leaves were on the turn, their delicate gold caught by the sun. On either side beyond the trees the land was becoming sparse. Rock showed through the rough grass, among the broom and the scrub. I glimpsed a row of beehives set out against a limestone spur, and soon afterwards, well back from the road, a Provençal farmhouse of rough honey-coloured stone under a russet roof, deeply furrowed and dipping with a triple row of tiles.

The road swung up. The view was

opening out. St Pierre-de-Lys was lost to sight. In the distance across another fold in the hills I could see another hilltop town, smaller than St Pierre-de-Lys, contained within its grim brown walls. Blue was deepening in the sky, with exquisite wisps of cloud lying above the higher hills to the north. A side-road came in, half hidden in a mass of scrub-oak and here Crispin drew up.

"This is where we found the car," he said. "I remember quite clearly driving to this point on the road. Now, where did I go from here?"

We got out and I looked about me. There was utter silence except for the incessant whirring of crickets. A light breeze rippled through the leaves of the trees from time to time. A wasp zoomed past. Bees were busy among the tiny flowering plants on the stony ground.

I said, "Crispin, I'm going to be no help to you at all. It was dark that night, raining as I said. We were tired. We had driven down from Paris, after all — "

"You were just arriving?"

"Yes. I was map-reading in a kind of a way. I remember after the last village there was an empty stretch of road and that sometimes we were rising and sometimes coming down, but beyond that — "

"Let's get the car round," said Crispin, "and we'll start on the way back. I'll take it slowly. Think yourself back to that night. There's a map on the shelf."

I did as he said, sitting forward and scanning the road as I had done that night. But it was all so totally different. Then it had been a black void, lashed with rain. Now the hot sun blazed down on a Mediterranean hillside.

"There's no feature that I could possibly remember," I said. "When you were trudging along I'd have said the road was level. I don't remember trees. That town across the gully — wouldn't there have been lights? Maybe there were and I didn't notice."

Crispin Lingard was disappointed and didn't pretend he wasn't. When we got

81

to the crest above St Pierre-de-Lys he turned about and drove back to the road junction where he had abandoned his car. "It's possible," he said, "that I started off walking the other way. After all, I was mildly off my head."

"But we overtook you from behind."

"I could have gone so far, though, and turned about — " He thrust a hand irritably into his hair. "Could you bear with me a little longer? Suppose we try a mile or two farther — "

He drove northwards fast for a few miles, put the car round and came slowly back towards the crossroads. There was a sign for the side-road but I had no memory of having seen it, either before or after we had stopped to pick him up.

"Well, thanks, Dinah," he said. "I'll take you back. I've been over the ground around the crossroads. I'll just have to keep at it, every inch of the wayside. At least I know for certain now that I was on the main road. On the left-hand side or the right?"

"The left."

"That's something, anyway."

"We could make a start now. I'd like to help — "

He smiled briefly and shook his head. "No way! Unless — "

"Yes?"

"You said you were travelling with your boss. Who is he?"

Why on earth did I have to redden? From guilt, because the same thought had occurred to me and I didn't want to raise it?

"He runs the Summer School at La Closerie."

"Oh lord! I suppose he knows people in St Pierre-de-Lys connected with the Festival?"

"I've no idea." Why should that matter?

"Could you possibly ask him if he remembers anything that could pinpoint where I was?"

I suppose I was overlong in answering. "Difficult, is he?"

"He has a lot to do — "

Crispin sighed. "Point taken! I'll do

my own dirty work!"

"Don't be absurd," I said. "I'll speak to him." I had wanted to in any case.

It was almost time for dinner at La Closerie and students and staff, showered and changed and relaxed, were sitting about at those little metal tables, sipping apéritifs. Dr Alexander was in the centre of a lively group. He saw me the minute I came in through the wrought-iron gate, but he made no sign. For a few minutes I hung about, hoping I might catch his eye. I could not bring myself to march right up to the table where he sat and interrupt. Then I gave up. I should have to go back to Crispin, tell him I would do what I could when I could, and that I'd ring him right away. I felt drained by the heat and the stresses of the day. It was hard to be misjudged.

I moved away, out of the courtyard's cool, into the glare of the street. The sun had gone down behind the high flats but the pavements and the buildings retained its fierce heat. Crispin had said he would wait for me in the café where earlier we had had a drink. He would be having another now.

I was a few yards along the pavement when Dr Alexander behind me said sharply, "Is anything the matter?"

He had come after me and was looking at me now, frowning in unconcealed irritation.

"If you wanted to speak to me," he said, "why didn't you come and do so?"

Which didn't make all that much sense. If he had guessed I wanted to speak to him, why hadn't he at least looked my way?

I leant against the railing to take the weight off my feet.

"I thought it wasn't convenient — "

"Not a consideration you've always worried about!"

I flushed. How was it that he and I struck sparks off each other so? He couldn't talk like that to his students or they wouldn't be so adoring!

I said, "The yob you gave the lift to that evening in the rain — he was the player in the concert last night who spoke to me — "

Dr Alexander's eyebrows were in their black straight line.

"He had been in an accident that night and was concussed when we picked him up. His wallet is missing and he's trying to trace it."

"Does he suggest *we* took it?"

I stared at him. Was communication never to be possible with this man! "For heaven's sake," I said, from misery over burning feet and aching head, "don't *bother*!" I prised myself off the railings and walked off fast. If Crispin would let me help I'd go with him. At least he was human —

"Dinah!" Dr Alexander overtook me and had me by the arm. "I'm sorry! Really sorry. I'd thought, you see — Oh, never mind what I thought! Look, come back with me now and after dinner you can tell me all about this — "

I stared at him dully. "Crispin is waiting for me."

"Crispin?"

"The yob who plays the viola da gamba."

"Will you stop baiting me! All right. I thought he was a hitch-hiker. I used to hitch myself in an earlier life, but since then — Anyway, where is he now, this musician who has lost his wallet?"

I explained the situation as succinctly as I could.

As I talked we had been walking on and now in sight of the café I could see Crispin at a table with a couple of tall drinks in front of him. One of them — if chivalry wasn't dead — might be for me.

"There he is."

Dr Alexander gazed across the oleanders decorating the central reserve and said, "I wouldn't have known him. I hardly saw him that night in the car. But I might be able to help. I can see he wants to get back up there before the light goes, but I'll have to let them know at La Closerie that I'll be missing dinner. You too."

I said, "I wasn't suggesting — "

"Go along and join your friend. I'll be

with you in a couple of minutes. We'll eat later."

Dr Alexander sat in the front and as Crispin drove fast up the hill past the fine villas the two men talked, but I couldn't hear much that was said. The hill country looked more beautiful than before. The sun hung just above the hills now, the sky all around flushed with pale gold. In the distance, when I looked back, I saw for the first time the sea like molten metal in the light. The hills lay in folds, each fold fainter than the other until at the last hill and sky almost seemed to fuse.

At the crossroads Crispin turned the car and proceeded to drive back. We had gone some distance and any hope I had felt was fading when suddenly Dr Alexander said, "There you are!"

I leant forward eagerly. "What is it?"

"You remember I swerved?" he said. "The rain was coming down in sheets and I thought — " he smiled wryly at Crispin" — you were going to step out right in front of me. That boulder loomed up in the headlights and I just missed it!"

'That boulder' was a large piece of limestone, worn with the weather into a grotesque shape like something a trendy sculptor might produce and label Nightmare.

We all got out. Crispin looked back. "I'd certainly come some way."

"How is it we didn't notice your car?"

Crispin said, "It ended up among those trees at the junction."

"You went off the road? These surfaces are treacherous in rain. No damage?"

"None to the car." Crispin looked at his watch. "Would you like me to drop you back in St Pierre-de-Lys? You've been most kind — "

"Heavens, no!" Dr Alexander looked shocked at the idea. "We make a start to the search right now, while the light lasts. I suggest we divide up the stretch of roadside. This wallet — what does it look like?"

Crispin was looking gloomy now. "Always supposing it's still here. A very ordinary brown leather wallet, shabby — "

We spread out and for the next half-hour we went diligently over the roadside verge between the crossroads and the boulder. In the excitement of the search I had forgotten about my aching feet and head. The air was warm and heady with the scent of lavender and sage and rosemary. Tiny butterflies in blue and red flitted in and out of the spiky grasses. I found autumn crocus flowering among the stones. The sun dropped behind the hills. Almost at once darkness began to fall. It was days now since Crispin had dropped his wallet. What chance, realistically, had we of finding it? At least we had done what we could to help him. I drew near him at the end of my section, my eyes straining now in the dusk. He was downcast. I could see his hands clenched. Obviously, whatever had been in the wallet was important to him. And then suddenly he gave a great whoop.

I closed on him. From broken limestone

rubble overgrown with brambles I saw him take up something.

"*Crispin,* you've found it!"

His hand went thrusting inside the flap. As he had said the leather was worn and shabby. I felt his tension, and then visibly it went. His fingers had closed on something. He closed his eyes and let out a long breath.

Then he had flipped the wallet open and was running his hands through the separate compartments.

"Hell!" he said. "The money's gone!"

"Was there much?"

"Yes."

I watched him half draw out a photograph of a girl and then press it back. He took out what looked like a letter then, and tried flapping it open. It was sodden, the folds coming apart with difficulty. There were wavy marks where ink had dissolved in the rain and run. He gave a wry laugh.

"Symbolic, that!" he muttered. And then as Dr Alexander came up Crispin let the sheet of paper go. I saw it flutter to the limestone rubble and settle there, still soggy. Some words might have been decipherable, but he didn't seem to care.

"Am I right in thinking," said Dr Alexander, "that someone has been before us?"

"It would seem so."

"Money would be as sodden as that paper but I suppose anybody finding the wallet and taking the money could dry it out."

Crispin closed the wallet and put it in his pocket. "I don't know how to thank you for your help," he said.

"I just wish we could have got on to it sooner." Dr Alexander was concerned. "If I can help in any way, lend you something to tide you over — "

Crispin said, "Thanks. I ought to manage."

He drove fast back to St Pierre-de-Lys. Sitting in the back I couldn't be sure. He was preoccupied, worried. He had indicated that there was a considerable amount of money in his wallet. And yet he didn't give the impression of being sunk in gloom. There was a sense about him of deep satisfaction. I remembered his words: *That's how I could have lost her! She* had been in the wallet. *She* mattered a great deal more to him than the money, the loss of which was going to prove tiresome, awkward but not crushing. Was it the photograph of the girl? He hadn't lingered over it, but then he might not have wanted anyone to see. There had been something before he found the photograph, something his fingers had sought for before he opened it . . .

At La Closerie Crispin embarked on more speeches of thanks but Dr Alexander cut him short. "I'm only too thankful we were able to help," he said. "It makes me feel a little less awful about turfing you out into the street that night. It never entered my head you'd had a knock. We had been driving all day, past noticing much. Dinah was concerned, would have preached me a sermon on charity if I had let her!"

I blushed furiously. Dr Alexander was smiling at me quizzically. Crispin caught my hand and kissed the palm, closing my fingers over it. "Bless you," he said for the second time that day. "Now I must let you go. But I'll be seeing you soon!" It was a statement, not a question.

In the kitchen they had kept dinner for us, *potage, boeuf provençale,* side salad with cheese to follow. Dr Alexander ordered a bottle of red wine and topped up my glass whenever the level lowered.

It had been heaven to shower and change. Now, it was bliss to relax in the cool refectory after the busy day and our exertion up in the hills. We talked about Crispin at first, speculating on his accident, neither of us having cared to probe, wondering just how much money he had lost.

"That car cost a packet," Dr Alexander said. "It would look as though he is pretty well-heeled."

"So whatever went missing isn't going to break him."

"I should say not. And he didn't really

seem unduly worried."

"That was my impression too."

We moved on after that, talking easily as people do who know each other well. We touched on things connected with the Summer School. We talked about wine. He claimed not to be knowledgeable, everything he said pointing to the contrary. Once or twice he would have got on to music but I wasn't so mellow with the wine that I didn't see in time and change direction. It wouldn't do to be found out so soon!

When we got to the coffee stage he said, "Let's go out of doors." I was sorry our tête-à-tête was over. I had been so happy sitting there, talking with him, no longer sparring. But he led the way not to the main courtyard of La Closerie but to a little private garden that I hadn't seen before. It was hedged about with privet and laurel and hibiscus. There were the usual geraniums in pots and a lot of flowers I didn't know the names of. From here there was a view towards the old town.

I lay back in one of the chaises-longues. "It's beautiful!"

"St Pierre-de-Lys," he murmured. "I love it. The Romans founded it — no, the Greeks! On top of the hill for there was marsh down here in the plain. It began as a perched village — They're all over Provence. That's the technical name for them, did you know? Think of the history it has witnessed — two and a half thousand years — "

"Up in the old town," I said dreamily, "you can feel you're back — with monks in La Closerie, friars in the streets and minstrels and knights whooping it up after a stint at the Crusades!"

He lay back and laughed, clasping his hands behind his head. He must have shaved when he had changed, for there was no hint of shadow on upper lip or chin. It was the first time I had seen him really relaxed. In spite of all that had gone before he was easy to be with. I was seeing now why his students adored him. He inspired confidence from a quiet inner strength. He would be unsparing of himself. Silence fell between us and it was easy too. I surprised in myself a fierce wish that this moment could last for always —

"Dinah," he said suddenly, "I owe you an apology."

"Oh." I didn't want him to go on.

He said, "You remember, at Bexton, when you came to see me — "

"Please, it doesn't matter."

"I was pretty unpleasant. I'm terribly conservative. I hate changes — "

"I understand all that. Miss Bowden's a honey. She knew the job."

"I taunted you about wanting the job for reasons of your own — "

I stiffened in my chair.

"Last night when dear old Mrs Benson said you knew one of the players at the baroque concert I thought that, after all, my suspicion was right. And I was mad. Dinah — "

"Yes?"

He turned over on his side facing me. "I'm sorry."

I avoided his eyes. It was dusk now,

but light from some upper room caught his face where he lay.

He said, "Look at me."

Unwillingly I raised my eyes to his. He said, "Tell me you aren't vexed with me. I'm not normally a suspicious man."

"You had every reason to be."

"No! There was a perfectly straightforward explanation for the player in the concert speaking to you. There could have been other explanations, simpler ones — It was preposterous on my part."

"Not preposterous, I'm afraid, perspicacious."

His dark eyes narrowed. "What?"

"I did come after the job for personal reasons. I mean — there is someone here I badly wanted to see."

I hadn't appreciated how much his face had softened. With its hardening again now I realised with a jab of pain what I was losing.

He said, "Go on." He spoke brusquely not only because he minded being used but because he had let down his defences unwisely and too soon.

98

"I wanted to see my sister," I said.

"Your *sister*?"

Obviously he had been imagining another sort of relationship where my attitude to my work could have been unreliable.

"Why didn't you tell me you had a sister in St Pierre-de-Lys?"

"If you remember, you made it pretty difficult for me to tell you anything that day."

He lay back, easy again, grinning. "*Touché!* Although you stood your ground jolly well." He rolled back to face me. "And have you managed to see her yet?"

"No."

"How's that?"

"Well, last night I was planning to — "

"Mrs Benson! And now tonight that baroque bloke and his wallet. You must feel the gods have got it in for you! Come on! Where does she live? I have the car at the back here. St Pierre-de-Lys is sizeable and it's getting late. I'll run you there."

"That's very kind of you," I said. "But really it's just as easy to walk. She's in the old town, up near the top."

"*Really?*"

"She runs an art gallery."

"What's her name?"

"Mrs Pearson. Melanie — "

"*Melanie!*" He sat upright and for a moment I thought the spindly chair might collapse. "You don't mean your sister is Melanie, *Chez Melanie?*"

I stared at him. "Yes. I always thought it sounded more like a hairdresser's. You mean you *know* her?"

"I'm in her debt. I've been coming here for several years now and every year I treat myself to a picture. Last year I came across a watercolour of hers that I really liked. She wouldn't let me have it as it was. The frame was wrong for it, she said. The border wasn't the proper width. She insisted on having it reframed for me at no charge to me. It's beautiful. One of my most prized possessions. Melanie is your sister. Heavens, Dinah, what are we waiting for? Come on!"

4

HE was on his feet on the instant, drawing me to mine. It could make easy what I had been dreading, the moment of meeting Melanie after her telephone quarrel with our mother and her harsh decision not to come to Julie's wedding. And then he let my hand go.

"But that's absurd, of course! You haven't seen your sister yet. You don't want strangers there!"

"I'd love you to come," I said. "She'd love to see you — "

"She won't even remember me. I'll walk you there. You can cope with wolf whistles, I know, but — "

"Look, I'd really like you to come. I haven't seen Melanie for a long time. She doesn't know I'm coming."

"How is that?"

"I didn't know I was going to land this

job, did I? Since then I've been busy." A lame story, but the best I could do!

We fought our way along the crowded pavements of the new town. Once through the great gate in the old walls we were in another world. The lights were paler here so that, overhead, you could see the stars. Voices in different languages reverberated from the high walls. The street we followed led steeply up. Music came in bursts from open doors. On some steps between the walls and crowding old houses I stumbled and he caught my arm. His hand was warm and strong. I was sorry when we gained a level stretch and he let my arm go. At the fountain where the geraniums rioted among the vines and the spiralling points of water sparkled like diamonds in the light he stopped.

"I'll wait here for a bit," he said. "If you don't come back I'll know that you've found your sister at home."

"It's difficult to explain, but, actually, I'd prefer it if you came."

He looked at me searchingly and then

he smiled. "All right, then! And that way I can walk you safely back!"

We crossed the cobbles to where some steps led down to the door of the *atelier*. The windows were lit, set with pictures, pottery and some jewellery made from local polished stones. Nervous now, I led the way down and pushed open the door. I had forgotten she had fixed an absurd bell that went clanging and echoing on the low ceiling. Almost at once there was a rush of feet and a little boy appeared. His hair was dark and curly, his eyes round and brown. A miniature Daniel! He wore pyjamas and had bare feet.

I said, "Hello, Jasper. I'll bet you don't know who I am!"

He stared frowning. Dr Alexander said, *"Bonsoir, mon gars!"*

Jasper's face creased in smiles. *"Bonsoir, m'sieur!"* He rattled on in French too fast for me to follow, but my companion understood and answered back and the little boy laughed once more. At that moment Melanie appeared. She was flushed and flustered and cross, her fair hair longer than I remembered, curling over her shoulders and half veiling her face. She wore a white blouse of some fine transparent stuff and a flowered skirt falling full from a wide belt.

She snatched up the child and with a muttered *"Un moment, s'il vous plaît"* to us she swept him through a door at the back.

Dr Alexander, embarrassed for me, was giving his full attention to a large oil painting that stood in a handsome frame on a stand. "This is very fine," he said.

"Is it?"

From the back room came a protesting yell from Jasper. I could hear Melanie talking fast but not what she was saying. Obviously Jasper was still proving to be a handful.

"It *is* very fine." Dr Alexander was standing back from the picture now, cocking his head from one side to the other.

I looked at it dully. Life was no bed of

roses for Melanie. I could see now why Mother had been so worried. This old house that I had thought romantic must be a nightmare to maintain. How could she run the *atelier* and do some painting of her own and cope with Jasper? "What's it supposed to be?"

There was a lot of blue and a lot of white and a general drift of pinky grey but no shapes that I could discern.

Dr Alexander laughed. "Obviously you are more into baroque music than art!"

Almost I said *"What?"* but stopped myself in time. Then at the bottom right-hand corner of the canvas I saw a strident signature that was familiar. *"Daniel!"*

He followed my glance. "Why yes, of course! This Daniel is an up-and-coming man, making quite a name for himself in Paris. No, Dinah, you don't ask what a picture is supposed to *be*. It speaks for itself, it makes its own statement. You can analyse the technique if you like, the way you talk your jargon in music, that's incomprehensible to outsiders, but you

105

don't have to! Just look at it, and see it for what it is!"

"Bravo!" Behind us Melanie spoke, laughing and clapping her hands. I wheeled round. She had drawn a comb through her hair. Now I could see she wore lipstick and eye make-up and in the lamplight her face had a softer loveliness than I remembered. She might be harassed, she might have her worries, but she hadn't hardened.

"What can I show you?" she asked Dr Alexander.

He laughed. "I think it's more 'What can I show you'!"

She frowned prettily, her short upper lip showing pearly teeth. "I remember you," she said. "You bought an *aquarelle* I'd done — olive trees below the old town."

I saw him flush with pleasure. "And you had it beautifully framed for me. I was just telling your sister — "

"My sister?" And then at last Melanie turned to me. I had been standing back, it was true, somewhat in shadow, and after

106

all she had no idea that I'd be turning up on her doorstep. She stared at me. I hadn't been altogether right about the hardness. It was there now, sharpening the prettily rounded features.

"*Dinah!*"

I said, "Hello."

"What are you doing here?"

Checking up on you, seeing just how you do live your life, hoping to take home some reassurance to our mother. "I'm working at the Summer School at La Closerie," I said.

She said, "Mother didn't mention you were doing this."

Dr Alexander came to my rescue. "It was all a last-minute business. We're lucky at the School, aren't we?"

After that everything became quite jolly. As soon as some people who had come into the *atelier* left, Melanie shut the heavy panelled door and slid the bolt. Lowering the lights she said, "Come through to the back!"

The room in the back was just as I remembered it, only now to the clutter of painting things and books was added the chaos of a boy's playthings. A railway track was half set up in a corner along with a jumble of engine and coaches. Melanie removed a plastic Sten gun from a chair and plumped up cushions before Dr Alexander could sit down.

"Café cognac?" she asked.

Dr Alexander said, "That would be marvellous."

She produced it as if from nowhere. "Now," she said, "let's get everything straight. I remember the *aquarelle* and the fun we had framing it, but I'm afraid I can't remember your name."

"Jon Alexander," he told her. "Without an 'h'. Short for Jonathan."

"Jon. I like that. And you're involved with the Summer School?"

Soon they were rattling on about the courses, the kind of people who came. "I'm afraid I don't bring you many customers," he said. "They tend not to have much money to spare, our students!" They discussed the Festival.

Melanie said, "It's good as always." She

had managed to get to several concerts. "A friend of mine is on the Committee — Raoul Grenier? They've had the usual hiccups, of course, last-minute crises. Henri Deloraine, for instance — down with a virus!" My attention sharpened. "They've had some odd bods standing in for him in the minor events so far, but for the big recital later it's a different matter — "

Did Dr Alexander take the point that Crispin Lingard was a stand-in, an odd bod? I glanced at him, but his smiling eyes were on Melanie. "And there's the singing competition, with excitement hotting up for the semi-final soon — "

It was a very long time before she paid much attention to me and then it was all very light and casual.

"Mum and Dad survive the great Event?" She laughed and turned back to Jon. "Our baby sister has just got herself married with all the trimmings. Poor Dinah had to endure the ritual — "

"It was a lovely wedding." I heard

myself priggish in defence of home values.

Melanie said, "I'm sure it was. Jasper enjoyed the icing from the cake."

"How is Jasper?"

"As you saw."

Jon Alexander was leafing through a folder of sketches to give us an illusion of privacy. But he had an acute ear for overtones. "That's an ambitious railway layout," he said, heaving himself out of his chair and moving over to the corner.

"*Don't* talk about that wretched train set!" Melanie scowled at me. "Dad brought it out last year — It was his when he was young and seemed to think that no boy should be without one. It's just too difficult for Jasper to cope with and he gets frantic with frustration when things don't do what they should! I'd gladly drop it over the ramparts!" Which would have been easy, for the room we sat in was built into the old walls, and the window looked out over a drop of thousands of feet.

Jon Alexander had squatted down

beside the miniature railway. "I wouldn't dream of touching anything when he isn't here," he said, "but I'd gladly look in some time and give him a hand."

Melanie said, "*Would* you?"

"I had a train set just like this. It kept me happy for years. I used to spend all my pocket money on extra coaches and sidings and signalling systems. I'm just like your father," he added with a laugh. "I've got it packed away safely for my son!"

"Have you got a son?" Melanie asked.

He straightened from where he had been squatting and went over to the deeply recessed window. "No," he said.

There was a moment's silence, after which Melanie and Jon both spoke at once, and then they were laughing and soon off again about the Festival.

It was late when we left. There had been more coffee, more cognac. Melanie had shown us some watercolours she had done recently. When, passing through the outer room on the way to the street door, Jon Alexander said, "It's quite something to have a picture by Daniel in your *atelier*," Melanie threw me a sardonic glance as if to say, *So you haven't been producing the family dirty linen in public! Do you imagine I'd care!*

On the doorstep she gave Jon both her hands and said, "Do please drop in any time. It would be wonderful for Jasper to have some help with that train! And I'd love to see you too!" To me she said, "I'm busy tomorrow night. The evening after that suit you?"

Making our way down the stepped street of old Pierre-de-Lys I felt the happiness of the earlier part of the evening had entirely drained away. Melanie had been charming to Dr Alexander but barely civil to me. She resented me, identifying me with home and family attitudes. She wasn't happy. In my first letter home to my mother I wouldn't be able to give reassurance on that score.

Dr Alexander had withdrawn. It was almost as if we were back on our former footing. When we did talk it was impersonally about trivial things, and we parted as soon as we got back to La Closerie.

Once more up in my room under the roof, gazing out across the valley at the sliver of moon, I was heavy hearted. I told myself it was because of Melanie and my parents' concern for her. But there was more to it than that.

Next morning I was surprised to find a glorious bunch of carnations in a jug on the desk in my office. More than surprised, I felt a shaft of happiness go through me such as I had never experienced in my life. He was sensitive. He had been aware of the undercurrents of family discord in my meeting with Melanie. He, too, had regretted the dissipating of the happiness we had shared over our meal and in the little side garden. I took up the card propped up against the jug with hands that trembled. What was happening to me? I opened the card, with its delicate coloured sketch of the *genêt*, the yellow broom. But it wasn't from Jon Alexander.

"To thank you once more, my Dinah, for your generous help and to hope you will have dinner with me tonight. Unless I hear to the contrary I shall call for you at half past seven. *Toujours à toi.* Crispin."

I lifted the carnations from my desk to a side-table. There they would be out of the hot sunlight and I shouldn't have to look at them. One of the maids came in smiling coyly.

"Mademoiselle a trouvé les fleurs? Il est galant, cet jeune homme, n'est-ce pas?"

I laughed. Oh, yes, Crispin was gallant, like the knights and the troubadours that went with his name!

Jon Alexander I didn't see until lunchtime when I encountered him in the queue.

He said, "I'm afraid I did rather butt in last night — the first time you had seen your sister."

"Don't worry about it!" I hadn't meant to snap, but my absurd emotions were not yet wholly under control. "We'll probably have a bit of a scrap tomorrow night and that will clear the air!"

He frowned. "A scrap?"

"It wasn't exactly all sweetness and light. Don't pretend you didn't notice!" I walked off with my tray, forgetting to collect something to drink, but I had spotted a vacant space at a table where I had friends. Already I had said more than I had meant to.

All morning I had planned that I would ring Crispin, thank him for the flowers and his invitation and explain that regretfully I couldn't accept. The day wore on, however, and I didn't make the phone call. I felt restless, churned up. I *had* given Crispin some help, after all, and it was nice of him to want to thank me. I remembered the photograph in the wallet. It was just possible that he was lonely, as I was.

I took great trouble over my hair and my face and put on what I considered my prettiest dress, a wispy thing in delicate green. I made sure I was out under the acacia trees well before dinner and settled myself at a table where Dr Alexander on a bench under the bougainvillea could see me. I was joined by one or two of the junior staff and, glass in hand, I chattered and laughed a lot. Not, I was sure, that it would matter to him in the very least. I had to do it for my pride. For some strange reason I felt wounded. It meant nothing to me that Crispin had sent me the flowers. It meant little that he was taking me out for the evening. But it did matter that I should seem to be having a rave time.

To my private delight the yellow car drew up at the gate of La Closerie well before half past seven and to a noisy exchange with my new friends I sauntered over the courtyard in my most elegant shoes and climbed into the opulent car.

Selfishly obsessed with my absurd and irrational wish to make an impression on Dr Alexander — as if I could possibly affect him in any way — I had completely left Crispin out of the picture. Now, for the evening, he was very much in it.

He was smartly dressed in a suit of fine light cloth with a dark shirt. His corn-coloured hair was beautifully styled. He took me to a restaurant, where we had drinks and dinner. Afterwards he insisted that we drive down to the coast to a little place where we could dance. The 'little place' proved to be flashy and sophisticated, where the price of the drinks he ordered made me wince.

I love dancing and had always thought of myself as good, but I had never danced with a partner like Crispin. Fast or slow numbers, he was the most stylish dancer on the floor. Never in my life had I danced so well. Conscious of eyes following us I thought, *This is how it must be on the stage!*

We didn't stay late. Crispin drove some little way along the coast road. I had a vivid impression of lights — in hotels and restaurants and festooned on boats bobbing in brilliant reflection on the water. He drew into a parking space and we got out.

"Let's walk along the sand," he said.

"I can't — not in these shoes!"

"Take them off!"

To cross from the road to a stretch of sand lying level in the faint moonlight we encountered stones. I hesitated, carefully testing my way with my toes. Before I knew what he was about, he had caught me up as if I'd been a feather and carried me over the patch of shingle to the sand.

"There!" He deposited me on the sand. But he didn't let me go. He drew me against him, holding me so that his head bent over mine. "Dinah," he whispered, "I've been wanting this since I first saw you!"

"That night in the car, d'you mean? All dripping wet?"

My attempt at sarcasm only made him laugh. "You know quite well what I mean. You're very lovely. But lots of people must have told you that."

Lots of people hadn't. Boys I had gone out with had kissed me, of course, but they had been inarticulate, shy of speaking the words of love. I wasn't

118

prepared for his kisses. I ought to have been, after his dancing. At first I made an attempt to free myself but his hold while seeming gentle was hard and strong. Fire ran along my veins. I relaxed in his arms and took his kisses. Behind me was the sighing of the sea. From somewhere beyond a fringe of pines, music came pounding a South American beat. His hands moved, drawing me still closer. I felt the hardness of his body, the urgency of his need for nearness. And suddenly my whole being was possessed by longing — *If this were Jon!*

For a minute more I stood there, drowning in physical pleasure in the arms of one man, dreaming of another, and then in utter self-disgust I thrust against his arms with all my strength. My movement had been so sudden, he had no longer been prepared for it, and I was free of him. I ran along the sand and he came after me. He caught up with me in seconds, but the spell was broken.

"No!" I said.

His arms round me now were gentle. He nuzzled my hair "You don't mean 'No'."

"I do, as it happens." He laughed in my ear. "Why are men so arrogant?"

He held me from him a little. My eyes had grown accustomed to the light from the young moon. He was smiling, disturbingly attractive, that crease deep in his cheek. "You do like me?"

"Of course I like you — as far as I know you!"

"Do you want to know me? Isn't it more exciting *not* to know the man who's kissing you?"

"I'm tired," I said. "It's been a marvellous evening, but I want to go back now."

"Not quite yet, Dinah."

Unwillingly I let him draw me by the hand towards the glitter path on the heaving sea. He stopped and took off his shoes and socks. Then he turned up the bottom of his elegant pants.

"Let's be little again," he said. "Let's paddle!" Hand in hand we splashed along the sea's edge where the water swept in on the sand with a lacy edge of white, to seep away with a rushing sigh.

"Would you like to be little again?" he asked.

"I'm not sure. Life wasn't all that simple then."

His warm hand tightened on mine. "You're right. There were pressures then too. And we hadn't learned how to hide."

"To hide?"

"Don't you hide, Dinah? From people, from life, from yourself even?"

"Oh, yes," I said "I hide." And he had forced me to knowledge that might have remained hidden or so nearly hidden that I could have pretended to myself.

"My feet are cold," I said. "Let's go."

He moved out of the water, but he held me along by the line of the sea. "Don't keep running away from me, Dinah. I want to talk to you. So terribly. I'm frightened."

"Frightened?"

"Petrified. At what I've done. At what

I'm planning to do."

Uneasiness crept in me like chill. I was intensely aware of the depth of the beach, the distance between the water where we walked and the nearest habitation. It was a restaurant, strung with coloured lights from which the music came in gusts on the summer wind. Cars flashed past on the road, but there were pine trees and broom thickets between. From the very first he had been odd, unpredictable. I remembered that first encounter in the black night in the rain —

I disengaged my hand and he laughed. It wasn't a gentle laugh. It was unexpectedly loud, and hard and bitter.

"Oh, the hell with it!" he said. "You want to go back. *So do I!* Your feet are cold. *So are mine!* But not to worry! Come on!"

He turned abruptly and led the way diagonally across the beach. We encountered a ditch with a runnel of water that was deeper than I judged and I floundered into it, soaking the hem of my precious dress. Scrambling out, I dropped one of my fine sandals. I cried, "Crispin!" but he didn't even look round. He found a way back to the car, skirting the shingle so that neither of us had to endure the indignity or discomfort that could have meant.

He unlocked the car door and held it open for me. I scrambled in. I expected him to put on his shoes and socks but he started up the engine, nosing the car out, waiting for a chance to swing round to the far side of the road. He saw my astonishment.

"Racing drivers drive in bare feet, or hadn't you heard? And for all you know, I could be a racing driver. Going on to Monte Carlo for a do-or-die stint on the track — "

He had the car round with a verve that left me quite ready to believe him.

"That," he said, "could explain the terror."

"Crispin, please, what is all this?"

He was driving much too fast. I had fastened the safety belt and sat taut with my fingers laced.

"Nothing that need concern you, my pretty little Dinah."

"Then why, back there on the beach — "

"Ah, then! Well, just for a mad minute I thought that perhaps you were a girl I could talk to. But girls in my experience are takers, and right now I need someone to give — "

"That isn't fair!"

He threw me a bitter glance. I had thought once before that he could look formidable. But for now he was at the wheel of a high-powered car.

"I wish you would cut your speed."

"So you, too, are getting a little taste of fear!" He laughed wryly, but he slowed down and in minutes he was flashing the indicator to turn off the coast road.

The road up to St Pierre-de-Lys was busy, with frequent intersections. He had to concentrate, watch out for traffic lights and careless pedestrians. There was a point I remembered from map-reading for my father where the road branched, and the sign for St Pierre-de-Lys was none too clear. By the time we were running along the contour of the hillside across the valley from the town he had recovered his usual suave manners.

"Forget all that, Dinah," he said. "I'm sorry."

"Something is wrong, though, Crispin. I'd like to help."

He put out a hand and closed it briefly over mine. "You've helped a lot already."

To find a wallet that had been rifled. "What you said about girls being takers — "

"I said, *forget it*!" There was an authority in his voice that I had to respect. Obviously he had been hurt. With the photograph in the wallet there had been the sodden letter. He had let it go, seeing its loss as symbolic.

If I had welcomed an audience when I left La Closerie I certainly was thankful not to have one now as I clambered out of the car, my pretty dress damp along the hem and crumpled from the car, my toes so gritty from the beach that I limped in my silly highheeled sandals. Crispin with no suggestion of our meeting again scarcely looked my way and the minute I had closed the car door shot off with a lift of the hand.

Mercifully, there was no sign of Jon Alexander. As soon as I reached the safety of the hall I took my sandals off and made my way towards the stairs in greater comfort. That was when I came face to face with him. What he thought of the damp wind-blown creature I had become, creeping to the stairs with my sandals in my hand, I couldn't tell.

What he said was, "Nice evening?"

I tossed back my hair and, for that silly pride of mine, I produced a radiant smile. "Marvellous, thanks!" I cried and ran on up the stairs.

Next morning in my office I found a single red rose in cellophane on my desk and an envelope which explained the dimpling smile on the face of the maid I had met in the passage.

The note read, "My Dinah, what am I to say to you, temperamental egoist that I am? Let me see you tonight so that I can explain. *A toi, jusqu'au mort.* Crispin."

Yours till death! In spite of everything I had to laugh. Before I started work I rang the telephone number he had given me and left a message for him that I was not free to meet him that evening. After that I concentrated all my attention on work. Word of the red rose, however, had got about, and at lunch-time I was teased about it and questioned about the night before. I made it all sound fun and got back to the haven of my office as soon as I could.

For most of the day Dr Alexander was closeted with some visiting French acadmics and I saw him alone for barely a minute late in the afternoon.

"My regards to your sister," he said. "I wish I was coming with you and escaping this lot!" The academics, I gathered, were trying company.

I had brought out a fcw English paperbacks for Melanie and with them and some sweets for Jasper, I set out straight after dinner for the old town. I hadn't slept very well the previous night, disturbed by Crispin's words and even more by the emotions he had revealed in me. About Crispin I didn't worry too much. As he had admitted in his note that morning he was temperamental. I did worry about the feelings for Jon Alexander that I had surprised in myself. He could well be a married man, although I had heard nothing of a wife and surely his many adoring students would have unearthed one if she existed. I remembered the enigmatic sighing remark of Madame Romain in Paris. Obviously there was or had been someone who mattered to him. What was equally obvious was that, no matter how I felt about him, there could never be the slightest question of his being interested in me. And, in any case, how could I possibly be in any way in love with him? From the very start we had not got on. He had shown his dislike of me and his distrust from the beginning. Things had improved certainly. I would have said we were on the way to being friends.

But love? Hot with shame I remembered Crispin's body against mine, Crispin's kisses and the intensity of my longing for Jon Alexander.

As I drew near the fountain in the old town, I found with some relief my thoughts switching to the meeting with Melanie that lay ahead. I didn't expect to enjoy it. The *atelier* was crowded when I arrived. A group of excited Germans stood in front of the painting by Daniel. I don't speak German but from their expressions it was easy to tell that they admired the picture. Melanie sounded as fluent in German as she was in French. She motioned to me to go through to the back while she attended to her clients. There I found Jasper in pyjamas kneeling over the old train set. He had been primed about me, for tonight he came up to me and said, "Hello, Aunt Dinah!"

He wasn't the sort of little boy you could hug first time you met and after two years this amounted for him to a first time.

"The man who came with you before

— Maman says he knows about trains."

"Dr Alexander," I said. "Yes. He had one too when he was a boy."

"And he's going to come and help me with this one. Maman just doesn't understand when it goes wrong."

I knelt beside him. I knew no more about trains than my sister, but I could remember being taken by my father to watch trains from a bridge in a park in Bexton.

"There were engines just like that when your Mummy and I were little," I said. "With steam and funnels. I remember going with my father — your Grandpa — to see the first diesel engines. We were so excited but he was sad. He loved the old steam engines. Some of them had names and were famous, like the Flying Scotsman."

Jasper sat back on his heels. "I have a picture in a book of the Flying Scotsman."

"When I was your age boys wanted to be engine drivers the way they want to be astronauts now."

And then Melanie came bustling back. There was coffee and Jasper was allowed to open the box of sweets and sit with us for a time while we chatted brightly about nothing. She wore a loose kaftan tonight in garish colours, with a lot of beads, and padded around in bare feet, her toenails painted scarlet. I wondered if she were making a special point of appearing *outrée* for my benefit.

When Jasper had consented to go to bed at last she dragged a pouffe over to the window seat, where I had curled up in the deep embrasure and said, "Well, this is quite a coincidence, isn't it?"

I hadn't worked out in advance what line I was going to take with Melanie. Now I found myself simply telling her the truth, with all the details as it had happened.

"Poor Mum," she muttered at the start. "But she ought to think for herself, not just side with *cc père de nôtre*."

"Don't be bitter about Dad, Melanie. You've got imagination. Try to see it his way!"

She gave an inelegant snort. "I can see it his way all too clearly, *chérie*. I was the apple of his eye, the genius of the family he bragged about at the Golf Club and Sunday mornings at the local. When his brilliant daughter went off to France to live in sin with a raffish painter he came a proper cropper! A lot of folks in Bexton must have loved Daniel!"

"Melanie, you are being absolutely horrid."

"Seeing straight, love. People are not all as nice as you."

"I'm not so very nice, as you put it. But I don't accept — "

"Dad's pride took one hell of a knock and he never forgave me. And it didn't occur to them how much that hurt me. I loved Daniel, after all. I admired him, believed in him. I knew he was a good painter and now everybody who is interested in art knows it too. He loved me, needed me. I knew nothing I could ever do in my life would equal giving to him what I had to give him then. But you haven't told me how come you got yourself here!"

She laughed like a drain about Dr Sandie.

"Dinah, *mon chou!* And then he found he was stuck with you! But he's gorgeous! Surely you aren't still smouldering?"

Not in the way she meant! "We get along," I said.

"It's amazing how things work out. I remember him so well from last year. He loved that watercolour of mine. It was good, the best I'd done for a long time, and I had been pretty ruthless about the price. But the framing had never pleased me. I loved him for loving something I'd done and cared about. Artists do, you know! What we produce is like a child to us. If he had been cool and impersonal and offhand — even though he paid me the lolly — I'd have let him have it with the frame it was in. But when he cared — I can see him yet, standing in front of that *aquarelle,* his dark eyes all soft and smiling — "

I got up and knelt on the window

seat. I could see him too! Across the gulch below the old walls lights twinkled from the villas scattered on the hills. One villa was as if it were floodlit. You could see the courtyard and the gardens, you could see into the lit rooms as if it were a toy model. Tiny people moved about in groups. They were having a party.

I said, "Mother was very upset about Raoul."

She got to her feet. "More coffee?"

"I'd love some."

She fetched the pot from a hotplate at the back of the room. "You haven't met Raoul."

"Shall I meet him?"

"Inevitably."

"Then you are still friends?"

"For heaven's sake, Dinah, we're civilized! And — work together in a sense. Sugar?"

I turned back and took the cup she held out to me.

"Mum and Dad liked him so much. They were so happy to think you were going to marry him."

134

She flopped back on the pouffe. "It would tidy everything up beautifully if I married him. He is smooth, a son-in-law you'd be proud to take anywhere. I could just imagine Dad introducing him all round and Raoul playing up like a dream — " She saw my face and stopped. "All right, Dinah, I'm hurting you, talking like this about parents you love. But you've gone their way, you've been a good little girl. You said something about imagination, seeing other people's way. Try to see it *my* way! They want me to marry Raoul because he has money, a beautiful house on the Riviera — "

"They want to see you secure and safe. They love you. Can't you understand that? They worry about you having it tough!"

She nodded, smiling in an oblique kind of way. "That's what they say. What they believe! But they haven't looked below the surface — ever! With Raoul I'd have been safe all right, another *thing* he coveted in a house full of beautiful things. I'd have had no worries over the *atelier* because he was planning to put a man in to run it. I'd have had no worries about Jasper, because Jasper was to be sent to school — "

Her eyes were very bright and just at first I didn't recognise the glitter of tears.

"But Jasper will have to go to school, Melanie. He can't — "

" — run wild around St Pierre-de-Lys for always. No, of course not! I'm not a fool. But Raoul doesn't like Jasper — "

I could understand that he mightn't. Rashly said, "He looks like Daniel."

"I'm glad of that."

"Oh, Melanie!" She had loved Daniel dearly. Did she love him still?

"Don't get sentimental, Dinah. Living in France, I've acquired some French characteristics and one thing French people are not — and that is sentimental. Daniel did what he had to do. He had to be free. I understand Daniel. And that is where Raoul made his mistake. He *forbade* me to see Daniel."

I stared at her. The picture in the *atelier*!

"Daniel came to see me and Jasper a few months back. He gave me a picture of his to sell. I could do with the money and I've been offered the price several times over, but — " She shrugged and laughed wryly. "Was I claiming I'm not sentimental? Don't worry, I'll sell it. To someone I take to — like your Dr Sandie! Anyway, when I told Raoul, he was absolutely furious. Said if I saw Daniel again it was off between us — the marriage we had planned as soon as my divorce was through! I don't intend to marry a man like that, Dinah, no way! The joke's on me, as it happens. Daniel is back in St Pierre-de-Lys with a one-man show for the Festival and he hasn't been to see me! Do you think he would mind," she said, "if *I* called him Dr Sandie?"

My mind whirled at her switch of thought.

"The *aquarelle* wasn't ready for him on the day I'd told him to come. It

137

was so hot, I remember, just before a thunderstorm. We sat on the rim of the fountain over there — " She nodded in the direction of the street. "Jasper was in the shop to call me if anyone came. But nobody did. The rest of the world was fast asleep. We talked about life, in an indirect sort of way. He needed to talk, I realised that. He was unhappy. I hope he's better now."

We parted well, Melanie and I. She hugged me by the fountain. "It's been good talking to you. I can't tell you how good! Come back soon — and bring Dr Sandie!"

My heart was very full as I made my way down the dark narrow streets. Melanie, our parents, Jon Alexander — all with their worlds of pain and griefs! I was hardly aware of the jostling youths, the impudent remarks that are thrown at a pretty girl walking alone in a place like St Pierre-de-Lys at night. In the courtyard of La Closerie a number of people still sat about under the acacias. Jon Alexander as if he had been watching out came to meet me.

"How was Melanie? And Jasper and his train?"

"Fine, thanks. Hoping to see you."

"No scrap after all?"

"What?" I said and then I remembered. "Of course not. I was being stupid. Families — you know how it is sometimes — "

He said, "Of course. I've got this for you."

From his pocket he brought out a little package wrapped in gold paper. "Crispin called."

"But I left word I wouldn't be in tonight."

Jon Alexander shrugged. From the few days we had been in France he already had a tan and with his dark colouring he might have been French. We were standing by one of the tables. Would he suggest a nightcap? Feeling as I did I wanted simply to be quietly in his company. But if I had practically forgotten the package in my hand, he hadn't.

His eyes were on it where it gleamed,

small and expensive-looking. He was frowning hard.

"I don't quite know what to say, to you, Dinah. In a sense it isn't any of my business — "

Wondering, I waited.

"Crispin Lingard. He has been taking you out in that flash car. I heard about the flowers he sends you. Now this — "

"What are you trying to say?"

He swallowed, avoiding my eyes. "I think you ought to know that tonight it was me he came to see — to borrow money. I realise he had his wallet cleaned out. But this was rather a lot of money."

5

THINKING about it into the night, I came to realize that it was shyness, embarrassment on my behalf that gave his voice the edge it had to it, but I didn't understand that at the time. Pride flashed in me like magnesium flame. His words echoed in my brain: 'taking you out in that flash car', 'flowers', 'Now this — ' My fingers clenched on the gilt-wrapped package.

"I've no doubt," I said in tones that positively rang, "that you took great pleasure in turning the request down!" and swept past him across the gravel to the entrance of La Closerie.

Upstairs, in a welter of emotion, I flung myself on my bed and burst into tears. What had I said? And *why?* For most probably Jon Alexander would have lent Crispin money. But I knew well enough why. It was his golden opinion I wanted, not pitying concern for a silly scrap of a girl running herself into trouble with an attractive lightweight. I remembered my flamboyant departure in the opulent car with shame, the humiliating encounter some hours later at the foot of the stairs. And Crispin! What was he involved in? The unease chilling me the night before gripped me again. He was in some kind of trouble. He had wanted to confide in me and I had failed him.

I sat up, turning over the gilt package in my wet hands. Short of money, *a lot of money,* why send me expensive presents? Instinct said, *Return this to him as it is. Don't open it.* But already the paper had begun to tear. Reluctantly I pressed the wrapping back. Inside was what I had feared, a jeweller's box. There was a note, too, folded round. Slightly sick I opened the box. On the white silk lining lay a sprig of real broom, *le genêt.* I laughed aloud in my relief.

'Dinah,' I read, *'je suis tout desolé* not to see you tonight. And tomorrow, my golden girl, I cannot see you. Nor the next night, nor the next. Put this on your pillow and let me kiss you in your dreams! Crispin.'

Next morning, having got myself sorted out, I came downstairs in a reasonably cheerful frame of mind. In my bag was the jeweller's box and the wilting sprig of broom. Like me, Jon Alexander would be reassured seeing it. Obviously Crispin's demands had been higher than Dr Alexander had anticipated when he had offered to help him out. And a man of sound sense, tight for money, wouldn't have been splashing around what he did have, taking a girl he hardly knew to expensive restaurants. But Crispin wasn't exactly a man of sound sense.

I had to consult Jon Alexander about a student's request to change a course and slipped along to his room between morning lectures. The sun poured through the window-panes, catching dust like dancing molecules in the concentrated shafts between the shadowed tracery. He had been scowling and when he saw me his expression didn't change. With him business always had to come first, and so I presented the student's completed forms.

"All right," he cut crisply into my explanation. "Leave it with me."

I opened my bag and took out the jeweller's box. "I'm sorry." I was breathless now. "I was rude last night. But I know you'd like to see what Crispin — "

"*No!*" His eyes met mine, hard with dislike. "I wouldn't!"

"But — "

"As I said, it is no business of mine — "

You made it your business, I wanted to say, *and I'm grateful. If I flared up last night it was in defence because I want you to respect me. Heaven help me, I want very much more than that —*

"Miss Heywood." His face was taut with anger. "I'm expecting a class."

Miss Heywood again! My control went. I snapped the jeweller's box open under his nose to reveal the sprig of wilting broom on its bed of silk. "*That* was what was inside," I said. "With a few kindly words. Nothing that cost a lot of money!"

I almost ran along the corridor to the safety of my office. If I walked out, they'd have to find someone else to do my job, wouldn't they? And somehow or other they'd get by. I started gathering up my personal belongings. I'd go up to the old town, have an hour or two with Melanie. And then I'd make my way to the coast. There was an airport at Nice, or I could take a train . . . Someone came in with a problem. Automatically I dealt with it. The phone rang. A group from the School had reserved tickets for a recital and the tickets had not been paid for. Almost before I knew it, it was lunchtime and a couple of the younger staff looked in to see if I was free to join them.

With people again, managing after all to get some food down, I was back to normal. The afternoon was busy and I hadn't a minute to spend on my own problems. It wasn't until I'd shut up shop, had a shower and was relaxing on my bed in my room under the roof that I could have a long cool look at my affairs.

I was worried about Crispin. I would have given much to be able to talk about him to Jon Alexander. How much money was 'a lot of money' in his terms? For how long had he wanted to borrow it? Had he given any sort of explanation? If indeed Jon Alexander had given Crispin the loan he had asked for — and I suspected now that he had — his bitterness at my reaction was only too easily understood. His concern, I had already perceived, was on my account He saw me as a wilful young fool, glamorised by, a good-looking escort in a flash car, and in his paternalistic way he saw himself as responsible for me. Hence his concern of the night before and hence my outraged response. For I wasn't glamorised by Crispin. When that good-looking young charmer had kissed me in the moon-light by the Mediterranean it was Jon Alexander I had been yearning for. Crispin's flowers and his blandishments had no substance and they meant nothing more to me than they were designed to mean.

In fact I was a sensible cool-headed, clear-sighted young woman who had fallen in love with a man in a million. The trouble was that the man in a million barely realized that I existed as a person. He had had some sorrow in his past. His life was filled, as far as I could make out, with work. He was seeking in his responsibilities for his students to find a substitute for lost personal happiness. As far as I did exist for him it was on the periphery of his life, first as a tiresome girl thrusting herself into a job when he didn't want her, now a potential cause of embarrassment and anxiety in St Pierre-de-Lys.

Self-pity swamped me and with it an awareness of sharp unhappiness. Badly wanting to be alone, I cut dinner at La Closerie and made my way up to the old town. This was not a time to call on Melanie. She would guess something was wrong and worm my miseries out of me, but not the whole story, and so she wouldn't be able to help. I had a meal at a brasserie with tables set out of doors under spreading plane trees slung with coloured lights. On each table a candle burned, thickened with runnels of many-coloured wax. Everything was rush and bustle, the *patron* and the waiter hard put to it to cope with trade. Dogs came trooping between the tables, grinning at being out on the loose. Boys on skateboards linked by string executed daring sorties among the tables to the noisy annoyance of diners. Above the chatter, bells from a nearby church rang out. Higher in the old town, bells from the Collegiate Church came like an echo, and every now and then an ice-cream machine at my elbow switched on with a great whoosh.

As I ate I went through a selection of folders I had in my bag about Festival events. Obviously it was too late now to get to a concert. And then among Art Exhibitions I found Daniel listed. His show was in the farther part of the old town, which I knew less well. I grubbed in that capacious bag for a street-map and decided I would have a try at finding it.

Finding the chapel where Daniel's one-man show was held took me the best part of the evening, and in spite of myself my spirits lifted. The old town vibrated with life. Young and old in that glorious climate were out of doors. I saw couples kissing, couples quarrelling, I saw children being cuddled and children being smacked. In any clear area of ground men played *boules.* Old women in black gossiped, younger women sat by their house doors working lace.

I don't know what I expected Daniel's exhibition to be like, certainly not the crowded, very efficiently run affair it proved to be. As I remembered, his canvases tended to be on a large scale, and an impressive show they made, skilfully lit on the rough walls. Two phases were apparent, one a sequence of pictures where a kalcidoscope of shapes in strident colour somehow suggested meaning, another of amorphic muted tones where no strong lines emerged, with any positive statement.

I walked round slowly, catalogue in hand, studying each picture in turn. For no reason that I could formulate I liked them. Deep down, each touched some chord, stirred emotion. I was totally absorbed when suddenly I caught sight of Daniel and for an odd moment I resisted the distraction of seeing him. For now the pictures were all. And then I watched him. The centre of a crowd, he was talking, using hands to extend words, like a Frenchman. He had scarcely changed. It was difficult to believe that that man was my brother-in-law — larger than life, as I had said to my mother, his thick black hair worn long under an absurd white straw hat, white pants and an immaculate white smock, his bare feet in sandals. I wondered who was keeping his smock immaculately white now. And to my dismay as I watched him he saw me.

I would have got lost in the crowd if I could, but he didn't give me the chance.

"Dinah!" he yelled over the respectfully

quiet crowd of picture-lovers, and in a minute he had pushed through to snatch both my hands in his. "How *nice*!" He kissed me on both cheeks and I caught a whiff of turpentine. "And what a surprise, my lovely little sister!"

I drew back. Almost. I was a sister no longer. It could be a matter of weeks now surely before the divorce went through.

"D'you like them, my pictures?"

I had to say "Yes", for I did like them. "But I don't know why. And I don't see any relation at all between the pictures and the names they have in this catalogue!"

He threw back his head and laughed. "Still my old Dinah! I think I'd like to paint you now. Before, you were at the kitten-puppy stage, not interesting to me — I mean, as a painter. All pretty and soft and unformed. But now the bones are clear — that lovely line of nose and chin! And those straight, uncompromising blue eyes — they haven't changed. Only just maybe you've lost illusion! Ah, well, that happens to us all! The names in the catalogue? What are you objecting to?" He stubbed a finger at the list. "*Sunset on the Nile.* That's how I saw it — copper sky, red hills, yellow sand, charcoal-grey water — "

I gazed at a picture I had especially liked. "It could be anywhere — "

"Not for me, it couldn't! You've got the past there, thousands and thousands of years of striving man, and a cruel terrain and the awareness of implacable gods — "

I giggled. "Sixteen we're talking about?"

"Yes."

"You could just as well say that of number twenty. And that's called Clapham Junction!"

"Life, my dear Dinah, is just as terrifying in Clapham — " and then he was laughing, catching me in the crook of his arm. "I put the shutters up quite soon. Will you wait for me? Have a bite to eat?"

"Thanks, Daniel, I've eaten. And I must be getting back. I'm not with Melanie — "

He didn't react at all when I spoke her name. What went on in the mind of a man like this? Did he think and feel like ordinary men? "I've been to see her, of course. I liked your picture. Actually, I'm working at the Summer School at La Closerie des Genêts. Which is a long way from here."

He looked about the chapel.

"They've sold, you know. The entire lot!"

I managed a smile. "That's nice."

"I'm not sure that it is. I'm not sure that I even care very much. It's all a damn circus, this — " He waved his arm to embrace the thinning crowd. "There's one in a hundred — less than that — in this bunch who knows or cares one damn thing about art — "

"You despised people in the early days too, when they *didn't* buy your pictures!"

"Despise! No, Dinah! Never say 'despise'! I don't *despise* people! I'm just dissatisfied with myself. What I really want to do, I can never *do.* The ideas my head is bursting with — Did you say she hasn't sold the picture?"

"Not when I was at the *atelier* the other day." He frowned.

"I think," I said, "that someone wants to talk to you."

"What?" He wheeled away to where a man had been hovering. Almost at once he plunged into voluble French. The Frenchman drew him over to a canvas, a tight knot of people gathered round. It was as good a moment as any to disappear and I slipped out of the chapel. I just hoped Melanie would not be vexed with me for having gone.

I have a temper that is over-quick to flare up and equally quick to subside. Making my way back to La Closerie that evening, my senses assailed on all sides by the sounds and smells and loveliness of St Pierre-de-Lys, I longed with all my being for everything to be 'all right'. For Daniel to be going home to Melanie and Jasper, for Crispin to be clear of trouble, above all for Jon Alexander to be as he had been those magic hours after we had helped Crispin find his wallet. But longing gets you nowhere. Daniel had said my eyes showed loss of illusion. Only weeks ago I had been mooning about my little sister marrying the handsome doctor I had had romantic dreams about — a far cry from what I felt now for Jon Alexander. This was real. Mysteriously I had grown up, become a woman. The next few weeks were going to be hard. I would have to work near him, to accept that he had formed an opinion of me that I shouldn't be able to change to any degree. Not that he would stay angry as he had been today. We would settle down to a mutual politeness no less hard to take. What to do about Crispin nagged me. He was no responsibility of mine. If he had got himself into some sort of a mess — gambling at the casino, betting on races or whatever — it wasn't my concern. And yet — once already he had cried out to me for help. *I'm frightened. Okay, your feet are cold. So are mine. You want to go back. So do I!*

Jon Alexander took longer to reach the politeness stage than I had bargained for. Any idea I might have had of discussing Crispin with him had to go by the board. In the days that followed it was as if he saw me only when it was absolutely unavoidable and he remained frigid. I was none too lucky in my attempts to see Melanie. She rang me, inviting me to a drinks party the following Sunday morning, and I said I'd also call in for a chat one evening during the week. On two occasions, however, I was asked at the last minute to organize groups to Festival concerts and when at last I had a free evening and made my way up to the *atelier* I found a young Frenchman in charge, who informed me that Melanie was out.

"*Avec un ami,*" he said, lifting his slim shoulders and flashing teeth that positively dazzled against his olive complexion. "English friend," he added.

"Well, *she* is English," I retorted. "Will she be back late?"

He lifted those shoulders again and

spread his hands. "*Qui sait?* He is a good-looker, the English friend!"

I wandered away from the *atelier,* pausing for a time to sit by the fountain. The water spiralled up into the light. I put out my hand and broke up the sparkling thread. I had counted on seeing Melanie tonight. The drinks party would give me no chance to see her properly. She had said nothing about my staying on afterwards. I had an idea she wanted to show me how bright her life was in this exotic old town in the south of France.

A short distance down the stepped street was an open-air café. I had walked up fast and was hot and thirsty. I sat down and ordered a coke.

High, dark houses rose above the cobbled street with shuttered windows under pantiled roofs. A bright display of ceramics spilled out from a ground-level shop. Everywhere therc wcrc flowers, cyclamen and chrysanthemums in pots, cactus, pampas grass, gladioli, orchids. Through the swelling talk I could hear the song-birds from their cages on the walls.

I don't know why I sat on. Maybe I had some idea that Melanie would come this way. After all, inasmuch as St Pierre-de-Lys had a main thoroughfare, this was it. When I did see her come walking out slowly from under a vaulting archway into the light, it hardly registered. And when I did realize the pretty woman in the flowered silk dress was my sister, I didn't see straight away who her companion was. Their heads were close together, she had her arm in his. They were talking and laughing with the ease of old friends. They passed a few yards from me, Melanie and Jon Alexander, neither of them glancing my way. For that much at least I was glad. Perhaps, remembering that day when he had come with me to the *atelier,* I ought to have expected it, but I hadn't.

Next day, Saturday, was the Summer School jolly, when more or less everybody joined in an outing by motor coach to some famous beauty spot. This year the trip was being made to the Gorge du Verdon, about thirty miles away. I had been looking forward to getting out into the countryside after being cooped up for so long in St Pierre-de-Lys, and had enjoyed typing up information sheets for the students.

'The Verdon river forms magnificent gorges in the limestone plateau of Upper Provence, of which the most striking is the Grand Canyon, over twenty-one kilometres long. The sight of this gigantic gully with its sheer rock sides is unrivalled in Europe . . . ' I had typed out details from guidebooks of the width of the gorge at top and bottom, the various depths, and a description of the route our coach would follow, with each viewpoint or Belvedere listed. There seemed to be dozens of these viewpoints: La Maline, the Belvedere of Samson Corridor, the Glacieres Belvedere, the Dent d'Aire, the Point Sublime. Warnings had had to be underlined on the typed sheets. Walking in the Grand Canyon was not within the compass of today's expedition. On no account should anyone leave the party and attempt a descent into the Canyon . . .

It was my responsibility to check that everybody was on the bus when we left and after every stop. Jon Alexander had asked staff to move around, sitting with different people for so long, rather than staying put with any one group. He was good about that. Students liked to feel that they all belonged, that there were no specially favoured 'cliques'. I was glad that the day was to be a full one. I had had a bad night, but I believed myself over the worst now. I told myself there was humour in my situation: Julie and David Parr, now Melanie and Jon Alexander. And I loved my sisters!

Moving about on the bus, chatting with the students, I was quite unable to wallow in self-pity. Everybody was in high spirits. The weather was glorious. As we rose above the coastal land we cleared the opaque heat haze that for so much of the time misted St Pierre-de-Lys, and climbed into a world of clear sun and brilliant blue sky. Plane trees gave way to chestnuts, turning gold now, starred with great conkers. Steeply sloping hills rose with sparse scrub sliced with runs of scree. This, I had typed on the note-sheets, was the Route Napoléon, the road Napoleon had taken on his way back from Elba for his Hundred Days that were to end with the Battle of Waterloo. Great vistas opened up at every turn of folding blue mountains. Broom splashed yellow by the roadside. Beehives were set in rows sheltered by patches of juniper and sage.

At one point on the mountain road the coach stopped so that we could look at a perfume distillery. Piles of lavender lay heaped on the ground. From copper vessels over a brick fire perfume was passed along pipes, distilled into cans and, overhead, great glass jars of several perfumes were supported on massive wooden racks. On all sides students clicked cameras before rushing over to a stall that did a roaring trade in selling tiny bottles of the distilled scent. I didn't join the rush to the shop, but lingered on beside the odd apparatus. I wasn't really looking at it or thinking about it when beside me Jon Alexander spoke.

"Absurd contraption, isn't it?"

I had been holding the wooden rail. My hands tightened.

"And all to make girls smell nice," I said.

I was aware of a sharp look but I didn't meet his glance.

"How is the train set?" I asked.

"Going round the track the way it should," he said.

"I hope Jasper was suitably appreciative."

"Of course he was!"

Of course! Jon Alexander would work miracles with Jasper too. He would have Jasper, like everyone else, eating out of his hand. So he had been to the *atelier!* But of course he had! Last night wasn't their first evening together.

"Can you suggest — ," he began and stopped. "That is, would you know

— what perfume does your sister like?"

The rough wood of the rail bit my palms. And I had thought my silly feelings under control! If he had bought me the tiniest phial of the cheapest brand I'd have cherished it for the rest of my life. But I had seen Melanie's dressing-table — why were men such fools! But that wasn't fair. Melanie might have received presents of Dior perfume from friends like Raoul Grenier but it was Daniel she had given herself to. She knew value when she met it —

"I haven't the slightest idea," I said and turned away to check the students trooping back to the bus.

The encounter with Jon Alexander had upset me and I stared at the mountain scenery with eyes that didn't see it. At the mountain resort of Castellane we stopped for a picnic lunch.

"If Napoleon stayed here, why not you?" demanded a travel poster and I felt lonelier than ever. Laughter is something you need to share. I didn't *want* to love this man! I didn't *want* to feel like this about anybody. I wanted just to be me, to get on with my ordinary humdrum little life —

I have no doubt that the Gorge du Verdon is one of the most exciting natural features of Europe. I still have all the data and the figures are impressive, but I was in no mood to enjoy it. I kept with people who were easy to be with, most of all Mrs Benson, who, in spite of her weak ankle, got out of the coach at every viewpoint, consulting her map and my notes and taking photographs with a little camera she carried slung on her wrist. It was a splendid day for photographs. The brilliant blue sky had acquired some spectacular white clouds that cast shadows on the walls of the gorge and the wild country that the tortuous gorge cut through.

It seemed that nobody could have enough of the gorge. Every viewpoint had some dramatic feature or splendid beauty that made it special. I grew tired. I was hot, longing to start the journey back. There was the feeling of thunder in the air that gave me the hint of a headache. When Mrs Benson, at what I believed to be the last belvedere, got out of the bus yet again with her friend Miss Tweedie dragging behind, I forced myself along too, giving her an arm on the rough ground. The last view down into the ravine was spectacular. From a slope that was gentle at first below the railing, the rock wall plunged to a distant depth where the river at the bottom looked like a snaking turquoise thread. Mrs Benson clicked away with the rest, but as luck would have it her film came to an end. She had a new one in her bag and proceeded to change it there and then.

"I shan't ever be back here, you see," she explained as I watched the rest of the party start towards the bus. "You will. Most of the others will if they want to — "

The film changed, she started on the next picture, flustered now because the others had moved off.

"It's all right," I said. "Take your time.

The bus won't go without us!"

I exchanged a smile with Miss Tweedie, who, lingering out of loyalty, wasn't going to break her heart if she didn't make it back to the Gorge du Verdon. We waited. Mrs Benson fiddled with her camera, trying for a shot that needed the lens hood fitted. As with the baroque concert she had a tendency to try for things just straining her capabilities. I wasn't watching all that closely. My feet were sore from gravel in my sandals and I was shaking it out when I heard her give a great cry, and I saw something flash on the wrong side of the rail.

"My camera!" she cried. "Oh, no! My camera!"

Hampered with other things in her hand, not realizing the strap hadn't been on her wrist since she changed the film, she had dropped the camera over the railing of the belvedere. From where we stood we could see nothing immediately below. I dashed along by the fence over the rocks until I could see what lay below. There was a grass-grown

166

outcrop that seemed to extend outwards and on either side for a fair distance. There was just a chance that the camera had landed on the projecting outcrop above the drop. I ran back to where Miss Tweedie was trying to comfort the sobbing Mrs Benson.

"It was a present," she said, "from all my friends in the village when I was able to get about again after my broken ankle. They said I could take pictures of the flowers in my garden. And I did. And last year I took photographs at La Closerie. And *this* year — "

"Miss Tweedie," I said, "get Mrs Benson back to the bus. Tell them I'll be along in a minute. There's quite a chance the camera hasn't fallen far — "

Miss Tweedie stared at me over her friend's shoulder. "You aren't going *over that railing*!"

"It's quite level for a bit. Don't worry! I won't do anything silly!"

I gave them both a little push and then dashed along by the fence to the point where I had noted it might be relatively easy to climb over. Once over the fence I found the ground rough but fairly level. What I did not like was the knowledge that it ended in a couple of yards and then there was the abyss.

Holding on to the railing I made my way up to the outward-facing side of the belvedere. This underside was pinned with concrete below the wall of handsome dressed stone. Other tourists had arrived. I could hear they were German, but I was invisible to them as they to me. From where I had judged Mrs Benson to have been standing I edged forwards on the grassy top of what looked an innocent knoll. But I had no knowledge of what it was like underneath. From what I had seen from all the series of belvederes we had stopped at and gazed from, the seemingly firm grassy stretch could be no more than an airy slice of grass-grown turf that would bend down gently when my weight came on it and send me catapulting down the eight hundred feet — or was it eighteen hundred feet here? I couldn't remember — of the Gorge du Verdon.

I was shaking rather badly, regretting my heroic impulse, when, a few yards ahead, lying cushioned against a mossy clump with some pretty pink long-stemmed flowers nodding in the wind, I saw Mrs Benson's camera. It could well be that the ground was as firm as Piccadilly and I had no more to do than to walk boldly forward. But I couldn't tell. Dropping on my hands and knees I inched forward. It seemed to me that the ground was bending downward in front of me, but that could, after all, be no more than the slope. I made quite good progress and had stopped shaking when suddenly the hand I moved to put my weight on went down eighteen inches. I screamed and for an instant felt I was in a forward somersault. When the world steadied I realized my arm had gone into a hole. Edging round it, I went forward again but the shaking didn't stop and, oddly, the sky when I looked at it seemed to be spinning.

Why I didn't stop then I don't know. It was as if all my life had been leading up to this moment, and the only goal the retrieving of Mrs Benson's camera. When finally my fingers touched it I lay flat on the ground and sank my face in the grass. Then it was as though the ground really did move beneath me. In panic I twisted my fingers in the wrist-strap and turned to face the return to the wall. I crawled my way up, scraping my knees and hands on stones and gravel. I was clinging to the turf, gulping air to steady my nerves when I heard running feet beyond the belvedere. The feet went past, along by the fence, and I saw Jon Alexander vault over and come scrambling down towards me.

"Be careful!" I yelled. "The ground's not safe!"

Near enough to the belvedere I dragged myself to my feet and then he had reached me and I saw his face. It was white, his blazing eyes black. I let out a long, shuddering breath.

"All right," I said. My head ached.

There was thunder on the way. Always thunder makes my head ache. "Go on, say it all! What were the rules about going into the Gorge? Do I realize what a nuisance I've been? There could have been a tragic accident! Etc. etc! Go on, Dr Alexander, let me have the lot! Then you can give me the sack!"

6

IT seemed that we remained there for an age, he white-faced and glaring, I drained of feeling. The sun was hot. The distant sound of voices emphasised the enormous silence hanging over the Gorge. And then he smiled and put out his hand. Probably he meant to take my arm, but I didn't think of, that. I gave him the camera. "I just hope it's all right."

"Damn the camera," he said.

He turned away then and led the way back to the rail. It annoyed me that my legs were wobbly and I needed help. From the rail over the rough ground to the bus he walked with my arm gripped in his.

"There's some brandy in the medical kit," he said. "I know I could do with a nip!"

"Heavens no! And please don't let

Mrs Benson think — I mean, there was absolutely nothing to it really!"

At the bus I got a heroine's welcome and I managed to clown it up convincingly. Mrs Benson wasn't so easy to quieten.

"You could have fallen," she said. "You could have been killed. I don't think I realised what you were going to do. But when I told Dr Alexander and I saw his face — "

I helped her on to the bus and found an expert on photography to examine the camera "Now, don't give it another thought. It really does seem not to have suffered. Where it landed the ground was mossy and soft — "

I had a moment's vision of that mossy knoll with the long-stemmed pink flowers casually nodding and regretted Jon Alexander's offer of brandy. He was behind me now.

"Come and sit here," he said, "where there's some air."

He sat down beside me, ignoring the rule that staff should mix and remained with me all the way to St Pierre-de-Lys.

He didn't say very much. I began to feel sleepy after the heat and the exertion and the emotions of a long day. Once or twice I caught my head slipping down towards his shoulder and sat upright in time. Then I jerked awake to find that this time I hadn't caught myself. Hot with embarrassment I sat up and then I realised his hand had been on mine. He had drawn it away, embarrassed too.

"You've torn a nail rather badly, did you notice? Will you be able to mend it for the party tomorrow morning?"

Well, of course he would be going to Melanie's party. I needn't feel surprise or hurt about that.

"Oh, yes," I said, examining the broken fingernail. "There are all sorts of things a girl can do to patch herself up!"

If only I knew how to patch up a heart!

"I would have suggested walking up together," he said, "but I'll be arriving late."

"That's all right," I assured him. I didn't want to be in his company a

174

minute more than I could help. This afternoon's adventure had set me back a long way. If only he had raged at me for foolhardiness! But he had had a real fright about Melanie's little sister!

I wasn't sure how to dress for Melanie's drinks party, whether to go all out on the little sister line or to aim at a measure of sophistication. I amused myself in the morning trying on some of the new things I had got and so far hadn't had a chance to wear. In the end I settled for a straight white sleeveless dress with a gold belt. Since I had been in France I had acquired a tan, and what had looked pallid at home looked dramatically different now.

The thunder I had sensed had broken in the night. Now St Pierre-de-Lys, watered and refreshed, was at its best. Outside the old walls flower-beds blazed with colour. Great plane trees spread shade, their leaves pale green touched with yellow, their bark spattered ochre, delicate blue-green and grey-green. Fruit stalls were massed with peaches and lemons and apples and pears, grapes and melons and peppers and aubergines. In the distance the mountains were already bleached in the sun, villas showing as dazzling white dots on nearer hillsides.

On a great sandy square men were seriously engaged on their Sunday morning game of *boules.* Older French women on social visits walked briskly by, immaculately dressed, with good shoes and bags. Tourists wandered about, looking grilled in shorts. A boy with a helmet nosed his motorbike through the crowd with half a dozen long French loaves in his saddlebag.

Melanie's place was already crowded when I got there. I had heard the swell of chatter from down the street. The olive-skinned youth was in charge of drinks. Jasper in little blue shorts and an absurd bow tie threaded his way among people offering savouries. He seemed twice his age, and was enjoying himself. Precocious child, like his father, that *enfant terrible!* And then Melanie saw me and descended on me.

"Dinah, *ma chérie*!" It was a two-way do, I decided. If I were to be dazzled by this glimpse of her set, they were to be impressed by the fact that she had a caring family. "Darling, you look stunning!"

"Don't overdo it. I washed my face."

"Come and meet everybody!" Meeting everybody meant that I met nobody really. I half heard names. Strangers mouthed at me and I mouthed back. The ceilings were low and it was impossible to catch more than one word in three. Melanie was wearing the flowered silk dress she had worn that night when I had seen her with Jon. Nothing too *outré* now! He wouldn't like it!

Her friends were a mixed lot. Some were casual, with a lot of gimmicky jewellery. Others were chic. A glorious redhead was eye-catching in snazzy black silk pants with a garish top, a fair girl exquisite in a long, flowered skirt with her golden back bare. Most flamboyant of all was an older woman in jeans with a red blouse and a great white straw hat trimmed with red chiffon. The men were mostly in trendy denims except one good-looking specimen who wore a beautifully cut suit in fine light grey. As we went round the room, my head beginning to spin with the heat and the noise and the drink, I wondered if Melanie weren't going to introduce me to him at all, but she was saving him until last. He was standing near the door where it was slightly cooler and you could hear.

"Dinah," she said, "this is Raoul Grenier."

He took my hand and bent his head over it, almost touching my fingers with his lips. *"Enchanté,"* he said.

"I'll leave you for now," Melanie said. "Must chase up Alain for more ice."

"And so," said Raoul Grenier, "we meet at last. I have heard so much about *la petite soeur.*"

I doubted if Melanie had ever spoken to him much about me, but could hardly say so. "I have heard a lot about you too," I said. "Our parents

178

enjoyed meeting you last summer when they were over."

"Ah, yes. And how, please, is your charming mother? And your father? And of course you have had a wedding in the family"

We moved out into the street and some other guests followed. It was a relief to breathe fresh air. He had a lean, clever face, with sharp, finely drawn nose and chin. His dark hair was cut in the French style, thick on top and layered, going down straight at the back. I could see that my parents would regard him as a sensible match. Very French, he gave the impression of being intelligent and shrewd. He would be efficient, reliable, everything that the irrepressible Daniel was not. But I could see why Melanie had reservations about marrying him. With his efficiency he could be cool.

Having satisfied himself on the well-being and prosperity of my family, he turned to the Festival.

"I hope you are attending our concerts and recitals?"

I was telling him about the concerts I had been to when I saw Jon Alexander arrive. He was dressed in dark slacks and a cream linen jacket and I thought I had never seen him look more attractive. He had brought flowers for Melanie which she received with a cry of delight, reaching up on tiptoe to fling her arms round his neck and kiss him. He reddened and Raoul's fine lips curled in distaste. I thought, *Melanie, stop playing one man off against another. If you only knew, I'm the one who is being hurt the most!* Jon Alexander and Raoul were introduced. We were all out of doors now, jockeying for places in an area of shade cast by a crenellated section of an old watch-tower in the walls.

Melanie drew Jon away to meet someone else and Raoul and I resumed our discussion of the Festival. He was enormously knowledgeable about everything, obviously involved in Festival affairs.

"The great excitement now is the semi-final of the singing competition tomorrow. Aspiring young singers from all over the world compete, not because of the prize itself — although it is much money — but for — What is the word? *Kudos!* We have many, many who apply and are heard and then they are-uprooted, yes?"

I smiled at him. He would have liked me to think his English was perfect. "Weeded out?"

"Weeded out!" He nodded. "Yes. Weeded out." Raoul Grenier would remember next time. "They are weeded out before the Festival. Two weeks ago we heard sixteen singers. All good — so very good. All of them will do well. But half of the sixteen had to be — *weeded out!* And now tomorrow we hear eight — four and then after an interval four more. It is wracking for the nerves. For the singers, I mean. The audience love it. It is such excitement! People listen. One says, 'I think X' and another says 'Impossible! Only Y can win!' *Eh bien,* each is good, so good!"

"It sounds marvellous," I said, "What

do they have to sing?"

"Here is always the great problem. Each singer chooses his own repertoire. Sometimes he or she chooses unwisely and gives himself or herself a handicap. Usually there is an aria from an opera, then some lieder — and at the end some lighter songs. It means for the singers much work, for each singer must present a different programme for each stage in the competition"

"You two," cried Melanie from across someone's shoulder, "are in quite a huddle!"

"Getting on," said Raoul coolly, "like a house on fire!"

It was then I decided that I positively liked him.

Melanie with Jon Alexander still in tow, slithered between a portly old man and a palm tree growing from a few inches of ground visible between worn old pavingstones.

"What are you talking about?" she demanded.

"Your sister is taking an interest in

the singing competition."

"Oh, *that*!" Melanie wrinkled up her nose. "The singing competition is a hobby-horse with Raoul!"

He stared at her, his fine-drawn brows down in a frown.

"A *what*?"

"Those idioms!" I giggled. "English is a dreadful language! Who do you think is going to win this year?"

"To win?" He drew a sheet of paper from his pocket and studied a typed list of names. "Now is too soon to say who will win. To go through to the final, to be one of the four — *c'est une autre chose.* There is a soprano from Germany, a fine French mezzo — " He tapped the paper with his finger. "There are two baritones who are sound. It is never possible to be sure. There is a tenor I would put money on — " He leant close so that I could see the typed names as a surge of guests came to Melanie to make noisy goodbyes. For politeness' sake I ran my eye down the list. The names could mean nothing to me. It was kind of him to share his enthusiasm. Possibly it was helping him too, if he had really cared about Melanie and was hurt at having lost her. And then I gasped.

"Crispin Lingard!"

He bent his head to mine. "You know him? This Crispin Lingard? The tenor I say I would put my money on — " He was gazing into my face and I could do nothing to stop the blood flooding my cheeks.

"Yes — " I started to explain but I wasn't given the chance. The departing guests had moved off. Melanie and Jon Alexander had turned back to us again.

Gripping me by the arm Raoul more or less thrust me in front of Melanie. "*Ecoutez bien! C'est merveilleux!* Your sister has a friend who is in the semi-final — not just anybody in the semi-final! The tenor who I myself think will win, Crispin Lingard, the Englishman — *He is Dinah's friend*!"

I saw the smile go from Jon Alexander's face. Melanie turned to him quickly. "That's the bloke"

She stopped, reddening. So he had told my sister about my gadding about in a flash car, receiving flowers from an irresponsible yob who then came to him borrowing money! I shut my mouth on the words, *I had no idea he was a singer!* At the same time I was beginning to understand something else — Crispin's terror. How much depended on his winning the competition? *Your feet are cold. So are mine.* Oh, Crispin! And these last days when he had said he couldn't see me he must have been working, practising, with the ordeal of the Festival semi-final ahead.

Raoul had been talking and I hadn't heard a word.

Melanie said sharply, "Why did you have to keep it to yourself?"

Stung, I looked at her. "Do *you* tell *me* everything?"

What I had said had come out simply as a cheap retort. I didn't expect the reaction I got. She went visibly pale and turned abruptly away. So it *was* serious between her and Jon!

Raoul said, "Would you?"

I forced myself to attend to what he said. "I'm sorry — "

"I have tickets much better for the semi-final than you will have. The poor competitors get free tickets for their friends but they are not the best seats. I would be charmed if you could come with me tomorrow as my guest, so that we may hear your friend win through to the Final together — "

"That's terribly kind of you," I muttered. I had no tickets. I had no idea when the first session started. "I'm not sure really that I can get away from work — "

Jon Alexander said, "Nonsense!" very loudly and crossly. "Of course you can get off work. Nobody is indispensable. What time does it start?"

Raoul explained the arrangements. Crispin, apparently, was in the second group of four.

"I tell you what!" cried Melanie. "*Let's all go!* Alain will mind the *atelier* and put Jasper to bed. Jon has said himself that nobody is indispensable, which means there can be no problem about him!"

Raoul was delighted. *"Magnifique!"*

Jon Alexander's eyes met mine. "All right," he said. "I'd be delighted to come and hear Crispin."

I made a move to leave soon after that.

Melanie said, "Must you really go? Jon has promised to set up that damn train set. It had to be packed away before the party. After that I'd thought we might go out, have a few hours on the beach. Have you seen the sea since you came?"

"I did check that it was there! I'd have loved to come, but I've promised to go out with someone."

Her eyes sharpened. "What's-his-name?"

Mrs Benson had asked me to join her for tea and gâteau at a little place she and her friend had discovered and I had been glad to accept as an alternative to just such an occasion as this promised to be, mooning round on a beach, playing gooseberry to Melanie and Jon Alexander.

"What's-his-name?"

She frowned, and then she shrugged. *Who am I to say anything*" About tomorrow," she said shortly. "It's full fig."

"I'll rub up the tiara!"

"Jon will bring you."

The following day I got more tense and excited with every hour that passed. Competitions always have this effect on me. I get worn out with emotion over Wimbledon. I found myself identifying with Crispin, trying to put myself in his shoes. I had no idea how he was living, who he had for company. I imagined him waking up to the thought: *It's today!* I pictured him going through the routine of dressing, breakfast . . . Would he spend hours practising or on the day of the competition have only a short session for loosening up? In the middle of typing notes I would go off on a dream of speculation.

He had talked so freely about his

musical family, about playing the cello, trying his hand at baroque instruments, and yet he had said nothing about singing, his real line. Raoul Grenier seemed to think he had a serious chance of winning the competition, which must mean that whatever happened, Crispin was good. But he himself wasn't so confident. If only I hadn't been a fool that night on the beach, made nervous by his kisses. If only I had let him confide in me — *I'm frightened.*

I remembered the photograph in his wallet. Did she passionately want his success? Was it for her that he had to win?

At last it was time to get ready. "Full fig," Melanie said, and so I put on the only long dress I had packed. It was in dark green, cut on severe lines with a skirt that hung straight in tiny folds. At the lunchbreak I had dashed out to a florist's in search of broom, but *le genêt* was not something one could buy commercially. When I found a stunted specimen in the gardens of La Closerie

I took it as a good omen and had no compunction in snapping off a spray which I pinned to my dress, the stem sealed in foil.

When I met Jon in the hall his eyes went straight to the flower:

"'Flower o' the broom,
Take away love and our earth is a tomb!'"

"Who said that?"

"An Italian painter, Fra Lippo Lippi — according to the poet Browning. Working for his patron Cosimo de Medici, painting saints, a monk himself through circumstances, caught out on the razzle —

"'Flower o' the clove,
All the Latin I construe is 'amo' I love!'"

We drove by the busy street under the old walls, in the welcome shade of the dappling plane trees. The concert hall was an ornate affair, in pink-washed stucco with elaborate carving. Inside, it was dim after the bright sunlight and blessedly cool.

We had missed the first two competitors. In a pause between items Jon found our seats in their favoured position and I sank down between Raoul and Melanie. The stage-set took me entirely by surprise. I had pictured the competition like musical festivals for children at home, with each competitor coming on stage and standing stiffly beside the piano on bare boards. Here, however, we had a drawing-room. The first four competitors were on stage together, sitting on elegant chairs, in gilt and green silk. The floor was of fine, polished wood, there was a magnificent grand piano. On little side-tables were arrangements of flowers and all was flooded with light from a splendid chandelier.

"It's lovely!" I gasped.

Raoul took my hand and lifted it halfway to his lips. Would he ever kiss it, I wondered.

"The girl with the long, dark hair has sung already. She is soprano. She did very well. Next the man — plump, is he not? But a good baritone. Now we have the mezzo-soprano. She is nervous, I think."

Beside me Melanie said, "Sssh!"

The mezzo had walked to her place beside the piano. Her accompanist played the opening bars. She was tall with a lot of light frizzy hair, in a fussy dress of muted colours. Raoul had passed me the programme he had been keeping for me. I didn't know what she was singing and I didn't like it. It was in French, an aria from Massenet's opera *Werther,* where a virtuous young wife Charlotte is besieged in love by the romantic Werther, not yielding to him but tempted. I stopped listening and looked about me, at the splendours of the hall and the glamorous audience. I located the panel of judges. The mezzo moved on to a group of German songs about woman's life and woman's love. They went on for a long time. I studied the man who still had to sing. An American, he was blond and tanned and athletic-looking, somewhat out of place in that drawing-room stage-set.

I applauded loudly when the French mezzo came to an end, from sheer relief more than anything else. Other people were applauding loudly too. Raoul was scribbling comments on his programme. He took the singing competition very seriously indeed. On my right Melanie and Jon had their heads close, whispering.

The blond American had a light, pleasant voice that was easy to listen to. He sang an aria from a Mozart opera that I wasn't familiar with, some lieder and then some light-hearted French songs. The audience liked him. Raoul, scribbling again, said, "Very nice. But for opera, no!"

"You mean you couldn't see him acting — managing duels with a cloak and a rapier?"

"For opera it is necessary also to act with the voice." He rose and drew me to my feet. "Now we have supper."

"I'll bet the singers will be ready for something!"

"Not those who have yet to sing," he said. "When you are to sing you have to eat well beforehand. Singing is not all a thing of the mind or the soul or the emotions, although these matter too. It is of the body, first and foremost. To sing you must be like the racehorse, the trained athlete. You must be strong! You must be tough!"

' He guided me down the hall, Melanie and Jon following, and by a side-door into an ante-room. Here tables were laid out with cutlery plates and wineglasses, with everywhere flowers.

"Is your friend Crispin tough?"

I had been pondering that very question. "Yes," I said. He would suffer from nerves, he would have his tensions and fierce anxieties, but he would bear them. More than once I had thought him formidable. He was intelligent, nimble-minded as well as sensitive. About his singing I had as yet no means of knowing, but he would be able to project himself, to act.

The buffet supper spread out on a long table in the next room was like something out of a book on hostess cookery.

"This is for nobs only," Melanie said. "Raoul is our nob. Not in music, of course, although he's passionately interested. He's on the art committees, but if you're a Festival nob, you're a Festival nob! I hear you liked Daniel's show."

Almost I choked on the chilled rosé wine. Melanie smiled wryly. "Did you prod him into dropping in on his ex?"

I found a ledge for the glass of wine. "*No!* It was pure chance that I went at all. I was at a loose end. I had hoped he wouldn't notice me. I didn't mention you — except to say I wasn't staying with you."

Melanie gave her snorting little laugh. "He was mad at me for not having sold his picture. 'If you don't want it,' said he, 'I'll take it back!' I told him, 'Maybe I'll hold on to it until you're broke again!'"

How they hurt each other, those two! She was wearing a black dress with no jewellery, drab against skin tanned from years in the South of France. She looked tired tonight, the effervescence of the previous days gone. My heart ached for her. If Jon Alexander really cared for Melanie and she for him, could I grudge her happiness after all she had been through?

Moving back to our seats in the hall I found myself beside Jon. "Nervous?" he asked.

I was, intensely, but I merely shrugged.

"I see Crispin is staying with your baroque," he went on.

Back in my seat between Raoul and Melanie, I studied the programme. Crispin was to start with an aria from *Acis and Galatea* by Handel. Handel's dates were given. Dying in 1759 he did of course belong to the baroque period. In my ignorance I hadn't realised that. To me Handel was simply Handel!

And then the chatter in the hall died away and a scatter of applause broke out as the second group of competitors came on to the platform. My heart was thumping, the programme shaking in my hand. Two girls, two men. I kept my eyes on Crispin as they bowed to the audience and then, smiling and bowing to one another, took their places in the elegant chairs. He looked relaxed, moved easily. But then they all did. It was part of their training. A girl from New Zealand sang first, a mezzo with a richer voice than the French girl who had sung earlier. She had chosen a favourite aria of mine, from *Aida,* where the Pharaoh's daughter gives vent to her bitter jealousy of the slave girl who has won the love of the hero Radames. I thrilled to the music, longing for her to go on rather than move to a cycle of French songs which were strange and didn't appeal to me. The applause I imagined was slighter than it had been for the previous singers, and yet personally I liked her voice. But they were knowledgeable, this audience, and were considering vocal technique, intonation, phrasing — If Jon Alexander but knew it, I was a total ignoramus!

And then my chest tightening I watched Crispin rise from his chair and come forward to take his place by the piano. Each singer had his or her own accompanist. Crispin's was a big-boned middle-aged woman in a sombre grey dress with severe grey hair. Her touch on the keys was magical, though, and in a few bars we were back in the days of snuff-taking gentlemen in powdered wigs. She threw Crispin an unsmiling glance and he smiled back. No one on the platform had his presence. It wasn't a matter of clothes or looks. He looked handsome. He was in something dark, I barely noticed what. But it was more than that. He had a kind of authority. I remembered what Raoul had said — 'like a trained athlete', a racehorse poised for the race. He was nervous. The adrenalin was flowing. But he was enjoying himself too. He loved being there. He loved to sing. And so his listeners would love to listen. And so it proved.

The glorious music soared, with the words in his fine tenor voice coming beautifully articulated and clear:

"Love in her eyes sits playing . . . "
Trills and repetition, instrument echoing voice delighted the ear . . . *"Love in her eyes sits playing, and sheds delicious death . . . "*

I found myself smiling at the fanciful imagery of the eighteenth-century poet. *"Love on her lips is straying, and warbling in her breath . . . "*

I knew enough to realise that it was not easy music to sing. With the aria's return to the opening lines there were further trills, then a falling cadence with long-held notes while the piano carried the melody. I hadn't heard it before, but by the closing moments I knew the melody would haunt me for a long time. The applause was rapturous. He bowed, bowed to his accompanist, bowed to the audience again. Raoul nudged me and smiled.

Then Crispin was preparing to sing again. Schubert songs this time, in

German, delicately sung with light and shade creating emotion even though I didn't know what the words were saying. To finish he turned to some English songs, in a different mood. There was less obvious artistry here. He seemed even to stand differently. His voice showed a strength that we hadn't heard before. The songs were about love, unrequited or betrayed, when his voice showed irony or a wry smiling at self, and then there was a lovely straightforward affirmation of love, a happy young man's song. It was a wonderful note to end on. The hall erupted into applause.

He didn't pretend not to be delighted. When he bowed he was smiling broadly with that attractive line creasing deep in his cheek. It must have been hard to follow Crispin and I was almost sorry for the heavily built German soprano who came forward after him. I needn't have been, however. Plain she might be, but she had a voice of such sheer beauty that while she sang it was as though everyone in the hall held their breath.

The final singer, a French baritone, was charming with a strong dramatic instinct. Raoul muttered, "He will go into some opera company, that one, and earn a nice living. But into the final, never! And he knows it."

After the singing there was a lengthy interval, when the singers disappeared from view and the audience moved about, eagerly discussing the chances of the competitors. About Crispin nobody had any doubt at all. Melanie, to whom Jon must have given the whole story, said,

"It's a blessing you picked him up that night in the rain. Otherwise he might have caught pneumonia!"

Jon, generous in his praise of Crispin's singing, was awkward and quiet. Did he have reservations about Crispin's character still? I was conscious of him all along watching me while I heard Crispin's praises extolled with flushed pride. Obviously he believed I had known about Crispin's being a singer, an entrant for the Festival competition, just as he believed I was knowledgeable about music. And things being as they were, there didn't seem much point in disillusioning him.

Excitement that had been electric all evening had built up to a tremendous tension by the time that at last judges and competitors trooped on to the drawing-room set on the platform. The four selected to proceed to the Final were announced in alphabetical order: the German soprano, Crispin Lingard, a baritone we had arrived too late to hear and to my astonishment — and no one else's — the French mezzo.

Each singer selected received a prize — handsome, according to Raoul — and a round of applause, and after that all order went, with candidates swamped by surging mobs of friends and well-wishers. I had expected that at this point we should leave, but Raoul Grenier had quite other ideas.

"*Eh bien*," he said, tucking my arm in his, "now you introduce me to your Crispin Lingard!"

I glanced back in panic for Melanie

and Jon. I didn't know Crispin all that well! He would have friends of his own round him, perhaps the girl whose photograph he carried in his wallet.

"I don't really think — I mean, some other time — "

But Raoul, as Melanie had told me, was masterful. Some technique of his with those high, slim shoulders had us cutting through the chattering crowds, and in no time we were at the foot of the platform. There were shallow steps between banked flowers and to my dismay I found myself stepping on to that polished floor, threading my way between bodies and those gilt and silk chairs. Melanie close behind me said, "There he is, by the piano!"

In total reluctance I hung back. Crispin hadn't seen me for days. It was quite possible that in the excitement of the evening and his success he wouldn't even remember who I was. Raoul propelled me forward in his iron grip. To be humiliated perhaps in front of him and Melanie and Jon Alexander! I wrenched myself free. I would not face Crispin now —

"*Dinah!*" A tenor's voice *fortissimo* can be heard over considerable noise. I relaxed with every appearance of rapture as I realised I wasn't going to lose face in front of Jon Alexander.

Crispin had left his crowding friends and in a couple of strides he had caught both my hands. "Darling!" he cried. "My darling Dinah! You came to hear me sing! *And you wore our flower!*"

7

THE next half-hour is a confused kaleidoscopic whirl in my memory of excited chatter and banter. I introduced Crispin to Melanie and to Raoul. Jon Alexander shook him warmly by the hand. Separated from my own party I found myself meeting some of the other singers, their friends, Crispin's friends. Champagne appeared from somewhere and I had a glass put in my hand. It was all very heady, in a cosmopolitan crowd. I was thankful when after a bit I found Raoul at my elbow.

"It is all very well for us," he said. "We have had supper. But this young man — when did he eat?"

Crispin laughed. "Not for years!"

"I think for now you have some food." Raoul fixed him with those shrewd eyes. "I want to talk to you. But this is not the time. The day after tomorrow we are *en fête*. I have some friends to my house for lunch. I am by the sea. We swim, we laze in the sun. Dinah will be there. You will join us, *hein*?"

It was the first I had heard of it. I had forgotten about the public holiday.

Crispin said, "Thanks, I'd love to come. There's nothing I'd rather do than swim and sunbathe, and with Dinah there!"

Everybody laughed. Raoul slipped him a card. "My name, where you find my house. *A bientôt*!"

Goodbyes were said. Automatically I was moving off beside Raoul. Crispin caught my hand.

"Aren't you going to look after me? Feed me, be nice to me?"

"But — your own friends — "

"I want only you with my nice juicy steak!"

"Don't be too late back!" Jon Alexander called.

Melanie, laughing, said, "Be good!"

They disappeared in the crowd. They had assumed from the start that I would be celebrating with Crispin.

He said, "My favourite restaurant is up on the ramparts. Come on!"

It was a relief to be out of the hall, drawing the evening air into my lungs. As always, everywhere in St Pierre-de-Lys there was the scent of flowers.

Crispin caught a cruising taxi and once inside he slumped. "Oh lord," he groaned.

Alone with him after all that had happened I had expected to feel shy, but I didn't. He leant back in his seat, closing his eyes. He reached out for my hand and I sat with him quiet while the taxi tore along the treelined boulevard and roared up into the twisting streets of the old town. There were the lights, the bright arty shops, the snatches of café music and the echoing voices.

He opened his eyes only when the taxi had drawn up outside a lighted doorway, and he made no objection while I settled with the driver. I led the way into the hotel. The dining-room was through to the back from the old narrow street, on a terrace built out in the ancient ramparts. A swarthy waiter showed us to a table for two by the half-wall. Above the low ledge, windows opened out under a sloping, timber roof with blackened beams and plants in pots hanging alongside lamps. Beyond the windows was a great void and, in the distance, dark against the summer night sky, was the mass of the hills, pointed with myriads of lights where the villas stood among their gardens.

The waiter brought elaborate menus and Crispin, casting off his languor, ordered a solid dinner of soup, fish and steak, with cheese and fruit to follow. He grinned. "Don't be too shocked. I can hardly eat at all on the day of a concert."

"Nerves?"

"Terrible! A lot of performers have. You'd wonder why we go on!" He persuaded me to have a salad.

"You wanted to tell me, that night, didn't you, about the competition?"

"And other things."

He was staring out into the airy space. I let my hand trail among the bougainvillaea on the window sill. For now he didn't want to talk.

His food arrived and I nibbled French bread and sipped some wine. By the time he had got to the meat course he leant across the table. "Hi there! I'm human again!" He touched my hand. "Tonight mattered a lot, Dinah. I've always wanted to sing. I've been having lessons for years. But everybody said, 'Great as a side-line, but for heaven's sake don't hope to make your living by it!'"

"That's when you did computing?"

"Very much against my will." He topped up my wineglass. "Don't get me wrong. I enjoyed college. I enjoyed getting a job, having a salary every month. For the first time in my life I could buy all the records I wanted and go to concerts — And I enjoyed life. I met a girl."

He was tucking in happily to his steak now —

"The one in the photograph — in your wallet?"

"So you noticed? Rosemary. She was a programmer in our outfit — pretty, fun to be with. I asked her to marry me and was thrilled to bits when she said 'Yes'. I'd slackened off the singing lessons at this time. I thought I was blissfully happy. We started looking around for a house, going to furniture sales. And then somehow — I don't know — I feel almost treacherous talking about it and yet I need to. It wasn't enough. I took up my lessons again. It was all very difficult. Fay Mellor, my singing teacher, is a dear woman — with a husband who doesn't deserve her. She never said I should go all out for singing as a career, although I asked her advice often enough. 'If you *can* be put off the idea,' she said, *'don't do it!'* And Rosemary did everything she could to put me off the idea. You can't blame her. I saw her point of view and I see it now. There's no security. Even if you make a go of it, it's no life! She wanted a home and kids and her man there evenings and weekends . . . "

Crispin pushed his plate away. He looked tired.

"We began having rows. We'd be asked to a party and then I'd get the chance of singing in a *Messiah* — somebody calling off with a sore throat. I was wretched and yet I couldn't help myself. One night she said, 'Okay, Caruso, it's me or your career!' and I said, 'Okay. If you put it like that, it's my career!' I threw up my job more or less next day. I'd been saving quite hard, thought I could live on my hump. I was getting a few engagements here and there. The Mellors have been coming out to St Pierre-de-Lys for a year or two. Fay has a friend here, a fellow singer from her younger days, who did rather better than Fay in the marriage stakes. He's in business, keen on music and I'm working for him as a kind of secretary-dogsbody over the Festival. The posh car is one of his!

"Mellor himself is a disaster. He was a clarinettist, then developed arthritis in his hands and took to drink. You feel sorry for him, of course, but he takes it out on Fay. He set up as a sort of dealer — antiques and bric-à-brac. Fay suggested I try for the competition at the Festival. The prize money is pretty super and if you do reasonably well you get engagements. She didn't believe I'd make the semi-finals, let alone the final! She played for me tonight but she slipped away the minute the results were announced."

I remembered the faded woman in grey. "She must be absolutely thrilled."

He frowned. "I don't know. We aren't pulling together so well these days. One is so terrifyingly alone — I'm sorry, Dinah. I'm being poor company tonight. Forgive me!" The waiter had placed a basket of fruit on the table. "Have a peach!"

The peaches were delicious, large and sweet with juice that dripped from the fingers and down our chins. He asked for finger-bowls and we dipped our hands in the water, giggling like school kids. Then, sitting back in his chair, he drew from an inside pocket the envelope he had received on the platform. He took out the citation and then the cheque. I didn't see how much it was for. He held it up with both hands and kissed it before putting it back in its envelope.

"It would be rather nice," he said, "to frame it. But I can't afford extravagant gestures. I'll be able to settle my debts."

The waiter had set the coffee jug before me and I poured out carefully. "Black or white?"

He was watching me, smiling. "I'm sober now, but I prefer black. I haven't told you how lovely you look tonight. The broom is wilting, though. Everything changes. Nothing remains the same. But I mustn't get maudlin." He took the cup I handed to him. "Dr Alexander will get his money in the morning. He would have been getting it tomorrow anyway. I'd arranged it with my bank. But I won't pretend this doesn't make things easier."

I pretended not to understand. Jon Alexander would not normally have said anything to me about Crispin's asking for a loan; it was that he was concerned that I should know what sort of character Crispin was!

Crispin said, "It was good of him, and he was very generous tonight. But he doesn't regard me as a very trustworthy person."

"Sugar?"

"And you aren't a very good actress, Dinah!"

"I'm not sure that I'm with you."

"Dr Alexander — worthy fellow that he is — hasn't he warned you *Beware the libertine*!"

"Dr Alexander has a job of work, Crispin, which he does very efficiently. I have a job too — "

"And there's no more to it than that?"

"What could there be?"

"If you were my secretary I'd be in love with you, madly. As I am in any case. He must have ice in his veins — "

"What about Rosemary?"

"Rosemary, ah!" He stirred sugar in

his coffee. "Love, it's so complex. What is it, Dinah, do you know?"

I thought I knew but I didn't want to talk about it.

"I doubt if I ever loved Rosemary. I was in love with a way of life, an image of safety and domesticity." He passed his cup across for more coffee. "That night when I was robbed I lost ten thousand francs."

"That much!" I splashed the coffee in his cup. "No wonder you were in a lather to find your wallet!"

And no wonder Jon Alexander had been concerned!

"It wasn't *my* money. Guy Mellor — he doesn't tell Fay what he's up to half the time and I can't. He hunts around for antiques, old pictures, anything he thinks will fetch a packet in that shop of his. The French country folk have all their back teeth and I doubt if many old crones have treasures they don't know the value of. But he'd come across an old engraved map in some out-of-the-way village. He'd negotiated the purchase

215

earlier but hadn't the money on him. And the night you picked me up I was on my way to settle and collect.

"I didn't tell you the truth about that night. I didn't have an accident. I was set upon — "

"Somebody knew you had all that money?"

"No. The money in my wallet was a bonus for them! I was followed from St Pierre-de-Lys by a couple of youths. They'd recognised the car. I'd annoyed them the night before. They beat me up."

"The graze on your face — "

He smiled wryly, touching his cheek. "Just as well they don't go in for the razor. It wouldn't have looked so good on that drawing-room set this evening, would it?'

"But Crispin, *why*?"

He shrugged. "It was at an open-air café. There was dancing. The pair of toughs were bothering a girl. She was French. I dare say she could have looked after herself. But she was pretty and I was feeling lonesome and did my Galahad act — " He laughed. "All right! I took her to a disco afterwards and we had a very nice time. What's wrong with that?"

"And those boys had it in for you? And got all that money? And nearly had Rosemary's photograph too."

He had loosened his collar and was struggling with something at his neck. "This is what I was really bothered about," he said. "Much more than Guy Mellor's francs."

Curious, I leant forward to see what he had drawn from inside his shirt, attached now to a fine strong cord. I had been so sure that night that there was something in the wallet that his fingers had seized on, and knowing that it was safe he had relaxed.

"I wasn't wearing it that night. The chain had broken. For safety I had put it in my wallet. I thought if I lost *that* — "

"What is it?"

He held it forward into the light,

a small coin or medallion in some dull metal.

"My good luck charm, my talisman. My grandfather gave it to me when I was about five. He had got it in Rome during the war. He said it was genuinely old, but I really wouldn't know. It's the head of St Cecilia, patron saint of music. The first time I wore it was when I auditioned for the cathedral choir. Always she has brought me luck — "

Our eyes met. His were very bright. He believed what he said. If he had lost his talisman he would not have got into the final of the competition because his confidence would have been destroyed and he wouldn't have sung well. It wouldn't do for me to laugh. But he laughed. "So I'm superstitious! That worries you, doesn't it? Because it's irrational."

"Not altogether. I do understand."

He tucked St Cecilia carefully away under his smart shirt. I wondered what Rosemary made of her — if she knew!

"The money, though," he said. "Mellor

didn't want Fay to know what he'd been up to and so I couldn't give the police the facts. I could have spotted these lads probably, but Mellor had me, for if Fay had got to know I'd been larking on the coast getting into fights over girls — She's a bit stuffy, is Fay. And I'd have hated to give her any idea that I wasn't taking the competition seriously! Mellor wanted his money back. He resents the trouble Fay takes with me and wouldn't have minded landing me in a mess with her. It was going to take time to organise it from the bank in England. And so I took up the kind offer your boss made. This Grenier bloke you were with tonight — how do you know him?"

"He's a friend of my sister who has an *atelier* here."

"The man I work for, Jean Dubois, has mentioned him."

"He's on Festival committees."

"And we're invited the day after tomorrow? What's he want to talk to me about?"

"I don't know."

Crispin leant out of the window and dropped a peach stone into the darkness. "That will fetch up somewhere hundreds of feet down. Leaves and dust will settle on it and who knows? Years from now a little peach tree will be growing there? And if it landed on a ledge that was big enough it might produce peaches some time — like those we ate tonight!"

I smiled.

"As likely," he said, "as my becoming an opera star."

"Is that what you want most."

His face was grave, with the strength I had glimpsed before. "Yes."

"I'd say your chances are a lot better than those of that peach stone!"

"My Dinah!" He moved his chair. "Would you think me rude if I said I'd like to get back now? I do want to see Fay — "

"Of course!" I signalled to the waiter. "Crispin, this is on me. I'd take it as a compliment."

He produced that heart-jerking smile of his. I could picture him as an opera star. "I could pay you much nicer compliments than that," he said. "And I shall! But thank you!"

Graceful. I doubted if, got up for the competition as he was, he would have a franc on him!

The Dubois home was on the outskirts of St Pierre-de-Lys in the opposite direction from La Closerie. We parted under the great gates in the ancient walls. "*A bientôt,*" he said, kissing my hand with expert gallantry. Then he unpinned the drooping *genêt* from my dress. "May I have this as a memento?"

I watched him walk smartly away. Yes, one day I should pay good money for a seat in the stalls to watch him kiss other ladies' hands, singing his heart out over them!

I got myself in my long dress back to La Closerie in a taxi.

As usual, students and staff were sitting with their glasses at the white metal tables in the courtyard, and somehow or other word had got about that I had a friend in the singing competition semi-final and that my friend had won through to the final round.

Mrs Benson caught me first. "That charming young man!" she cried. "And, you naughty girl, you didn't tell any of us that he was really a *singer* — "

A crowd gathered round. "They say he looks like being the winner!"

Jon Alexander came walking in at the gate. "Well, Dinah, you must be thrilled for Crispin! This calls for a drink!"

Everybody drank to Crispin, this young Englishman who looked like bringing us glory at the Festival. It was bitter-sweet after a time to find myself at a table with Jon. While generous about Crispin's success, he had not been fulsome.

"They say he's good, people who know."

"You mean Raoul?"

"And others."

There was something about him tonight that I couldn't quite define, an excitement combined with a kind of gravity. He would fall silent and then start to talk about the singing competition or something else, but I felt his mind was on none of that. Suddenly he said, "I don't see why I shouldn't tell you — " and my heart jerked. *No, Jon Alexander, not tonight. There's been enough. I know, but I don't want to hear you put it into words —*

I made as if to get up.

He said, "After we left Raoul, Melanie took me to see Daniel."

I sank back in my chair. My heart was racing and for a few moments I couldn't trust myself to speak. Melanie would want him to meet the man she had been married to before. She was open as the day. She would want him to understand.

Jon said, "He's quite a character."

"I like Daniel. I always did."

"Who wouldn't?"

"My parents. Melanie must have told you."

"Well, that was different. In their eyes Daniel ruined her life."

"She has survived. Given the chance, she'd do the same again."

"Dinah — I wanted to know — That is, how would you feel — "

At all costs he mustn't say more now! I gabbled, "That night at the *atelier* when you saw the painting, you didn't know then that she was married to Daniel?"

"Heavens no! I'd read about him in art magazines — "

"Don't think me rude." I got to my feet. "It's all been a bit much tonight, you see, the competition and the champagne and the excitement — "

He couldn't conceal the fact that he was disappointed. Here under the lights in the acacia trees with the roses drenching the night air with their heavy scent he had wanted to tell me he loved my sister. There was the sharpness of frustration in his eyes. Did he imagine I was too taken up with my own silly affairs to care about Melanie? But let him think what he liked!

"I did want to talk to you, Dinah. But now is not the moment. I do see that." He managed his avuncular smile. "I'm sorry. You're tired. And heavens — " he glanced at his watch " — it's much later than I thought. Get along to bed! Sleep well!"

With a feast day just ahead, the next day was busy. I had thought I might see Crispin but he didn't pay a call at my office, although someone reported having seen the opulent yellow car at the gate.

Arrangements for our visit to Raoul Grenier's villa had been left to Melanie, and in due course she rang me.

"Raoul has organised a friend to collect you and Crispin," she said. "Jon has been given instructions and he will bring me and Jasper. Don't dress up and be sure to bring swimming things."

Raoul's friend turned out to be feminine, tall, slim with sleek black hair and vivid make-up. She had collected Crispin before calling in at La Closerie and installed him in the front seat of her sleek white sports car.

"Deenah?" she greeted me. "'Allo. *Je m'appelle Louise. Je ne parle pas un mot de l'anglais!*" Not a word of English! But she had already discovered Crispin got along very well in French. Crispin in light slacks and a dark T-shirt exuded glowing health and spirits. He turned round from the passenger seat every now and then and called out something so that I shouldn't feel neglected, but the exquisite Louise drove with the sunroof open and the radio on, so I didn't have to do more than smile back.

The way to the coast was jammed with cars. The sun blazed down from a sky opaque with heat. The smell of melting tar rose from the road in sickening waves. Crawling through Cagnes-sur-Mer, cars jostling and nosing for position, we eventually reached the Autoroute, where Louise tossing francs into the basket at the *péage* put her foot down and roared along the fast lane. The motorway, a winding black ribbon strung with flashing cars, was bordered with olive trees and parasol pines. Scrub-covered hills rose on the right, with red Provençal roofs showing among cypress trees.

At the *sortie* for Fréjus-St Raphael

we left the Autoroute and plunged into an area where houses hid behind white walls, among acres of peach trees and vineyards. Then there were flats and hotels dazzling white like wedding cake and incongruously the ruins of a Roman aqueduct. By an avenue of interlacing plane trees we drove down to the sea. My first glimpse of the water was exhilarating, far out silkily blue and cool. Close to, however, the beach was crammed with tanned near-naked bodies under coloured sun umbrellas. Across the bay shimmered a little town with an enormous church, the harbour packed with yachts.

And then following the line of the coast we rose up on a headland of red rock. Louise turned down a branch road that almost I didn't notice, so well was it hidden among parasol pines, and a few minutes later we had arrived.

There can be nowhere in the world lovelier than the French Riviera if you are lucky enough to find an unspoiled spot, and Raoul Grenier had been lucky. His house was low, on three sides of a courtyard, with windows everywhere, well-tended flower-gardens stretching to wild woodland and a swimming-pool. It was built a little above a cove of unbelievably golden sand, between jutting arms of red porphyry, with the sea swaying lazily blue to the horizon. From nowhere could you see another habitation. You could have been on a desert island.

Raoul came smiling to meet us. Well used to the reactions of first-time guests, he stood chatting to Louise while Crispin and I gazed about us exclaiming.

Then he said, "The others have beaten you to it. They are already in the pool."

I have never been so thankful to get into water as I was that day. The pool was of an interesting design with skilfully arranged depths and shallows. Crispin made a spectacular dive. Melanie, nut-brown in a white bikini, was spread-eagled on her back out in the middle. Jon Alexander was holding Jasper's chin as that young man went through the movements of the breast stroke.

Raoul splashed Jasper making him flounder and splutter.

"Have a dip," he told Jon. "Jasper can have a lesson later."

"I want a lesson *now!*" Jasper cried. "Anyway, Jon can't swim."

Raoul raised his expressive brows. Stripped in trunks he was not so slender as clever tailoring had suggested. Beside him, although not so tanned, Jon was all lean muscle. "You do not swim?"

Jon shook his head. "So you could argue, Jasper, *mon ami,* that I'm not the man to teach you!"

"I want you to teach me all the same!" the child declared.

Lunch was a merry affair, served on a table set in the courtyard in shade. Afterwards nobody moved farther than to long chairs set out on the lawn, where we drank coffee and chatted drowsily. Even Jasper seemed content to relax, lying beside an exquisite long-haired hound of Raoul's that stretched panting on the grass.

Inevitably Jasper was the first to make

a move. Collecting bucket and spade he announced he was off to the beach. Melanie scrambled to her feet.

"Tiens!" From his chair Raoul protested. "Not to worry! He will be all right."

"The water shelves pretty steeply," she said.

Jon gathered up some towels and went off with her.

Raoul, his eyes closed, lifted his fine-drawn brows.

"Today she is all mother, that sister of yours."

I was nettled. "She cares for Jasper in the ways that matter."

"If she would cut his hair and teach him manners — But I am rude to my guests and that is unforgivable. Can I offer you more coffee, a liqueur? Crispin? Louise?"

Only Louise accepted something colourless in a glass. Raoul returned to his chair. "Now, Crispin, *mon ami,* this is as good a time as any. I wanted to discuss with you — "

Crispin had taken Jasper's place beside

the graceful dog that had moved a little way into deeper shade.

"This teacher you have — I think, frankly, she is no longer for you — "

What Crispin said I couldn't hear but he was protesting, all loyalty. He liked his Fay Mellor.

"Mais oui! Naturellement — " Raoul heard him out. "But now you are needing more. You are needing now things that this good lady cannot give you. I have friends here in St Pierre-de-Lys who know her well. After all, she is friend of Madame Dubois and *she* — "

Crispin hitched himself nearer Raoul's chair. "What are you suggesting I do?"

"I am not in music, *moi.* I tell you only what I am told by friends of mine who know. I ask them, you see. I make it my business. It is obvious you have great talent. What do you say in English — *potential*!"

Gravely Crispin said, "Thank you."

"My friends, they think you will sing in opera."

"That's what I want to do."

"And it is difficult. To get the small part here and there, to be in the chorus, and so to earn your bread — okay! But to do what you can do, to be a great artist, that is another matter! For that you must work. For that you have to study very hard. For that you need the right teacher at the right time! And for you the right time is *now*!"

I was watching Raoul. Even Louise who didn't understand a word of English was held by the drama of his words.

"Already at the competition you have caught the interest of several people. Believe me, it is imperative you move on. Already your good lady knows that. Already you have gone beyond her. But you must choose wisely and that is where I think I can help you. There is a man in Paris whom I know well. I want you to go and talk to him. For lessons he charges much. You will have to do work perhaps to make the money to live, for you must not leap into singing engagements before you are ready. That way you spoil the voice and you ruin your chance. You cannot overnight be a great singer. It is necessary to have much patience. I hear that already you are good musician. Already you have for singing some technique, but you need much, much more. And you need to study interpretation, languages, different styles of singing, you need training for the body, for the stage — But see this man! I am writing to him. His advice will be invaluable. Listen to him! Do what he says!"

Crispin rolled away, running his hand down the sleeping dog's flanks. Raoul said nothing more. Among the flowers tiny insects buzzed. Seed pods popped on a bush nearby.

Louise said in French, "I don't know what that was all about, but it was fascinating. I'm going down to the beach now. Coming?"

Without being rude I could hardly refuse. In any case Crispin could well prefer to be alone with Raoul to discuss his future. I collected my towel and followed Louise. By the pool she picked up a couple of air-beds, passing one over to me to carry.

We made our way between the carefully tended flower-beds to the wild garden where trees and flowering shrubs gradually gave way to herbs and sea grass, and then we came out between the arms of rock enclosing the cove. Melanie was in the water with Jasper. Jon lay stretched half in shade, half in the sun. He lifted a hand lazily as Louise and I approached. She placed an air-bed beside him spread it with a towel and lay down, smearing herself liberally with sun-oil.

"It's very unusual," she said, "for a man not to swim."

Jon closed his eyes. "Is it?"

"I haven't met a man yet who didn't."

"Then this is a new experience for you," he said blandly.

I spread my towel on a rock, deciding that I didn't much care for Louise, and went to join Melanie and Jasper in the water.

"Maman won't take me out there where it's deep," he told me.

Melanie said, "Don't be tiresome!"

At the edge of the sand the sea was warm. It came curling gently in little waves. I should have liked to go out where the water was green but it would only discontent Jasper and so I stayed with them in the shallows, playing about, making a lot of noise. Soon afterwards Jon came walking down the beach.

Melanie grinned heartlessly. "Louise does tend to go all out for anything male in sight. I shouldn't take it at all personally!"

Jon splashed water over her and they collapsed together into a breaking wave. We made sand castles after that, until Crispin appeared. He was looking thoughtful and I wondered how he felt about Raoul's advice. He seemed restless, wandering off to clamber on the red rock, up the steep, sliced face, and then out along the jagged rib that ran out into the sea. From a point that looked like a pinhead to me where I watched from the beach he stood poised for a moment against the pearly sky and then dived into the sea.

Jasper gazed open-mouthed. "I want to do that," he said.

"So you shall, when you're older!"

"I want to go up there now."

Melanie shrugged. "Off you go, then!"

We sat in the lapping water while the child tried in vain to get himself up the rock face. A little way up he stuck.

Jon laughed. "He won't cry for help." He got up and sauntered over to the rock. I didn't wait to see how Jon coped. Crispin, treading water out in the cove, waved and called to me. I struck out to join him. Even where it was deep the water was still warm, trapped as it was between the sheltering arms of cliff. I turned over on my back and let the waves lift and drop me. Crispin dived under me and came up to clasp me against him, nuzzling my face.

"Hello, sea nymph."

"Hello, sea monster!"

He ducked me for that and we fooled about. Catching me from behind in a life-saving grip he towed me towards the sun-baked rock. There was a ledge I hadn't been able to see from the beach and panting we hauled ourselves on to it.

"Now I've got you in my lair."

There wasn't much room on his ledge and it was necessary for him to put his arms round me. "Unless I hold you really tight," he said, "you might drop off."

"Or escape."

He tossed his head, sending water spraying from his hair. "You wouldn't do that — from such a nice monster! Did you hear all that — what Raoul was saying?"

"Most of it. Do you mind?"

"I'm glad. How much does he really know, this Grenier bloke?"

"My sister thinks he's pretty sound."

He laid his cheek against mine. My skin burned from the sun and the sea-salt in his touch.

"Do you feel better now?" I asked him. "Not frightened any more?"

He drew me tighter. "Marginally better. It was being alone that got me, standing

237

out for something against everybody I cared for. Even Fay — "

"You're scared she'll be hurt if you go to another teacher?"

"We talked that night after I left you. She said more or less what Grenier has just said."

Without a word of warning he got to his feet. It was as if he couldn't remain still anywhere for long. I lost my balance and went down into the green translucent water and when I surfaced he was already halfway back to the beach. I swam ashore slowly. Jasper had got hold of an air-bed and was trying to persuade someone to take him out on it. I heard Crispin say, "Okay, but I'm to be captain."

I hauled myself up on the burning sand and collapsed beside Melanie and Jon. Melanie said, "That's very gallant of your Crispin."

He wasn't *my* Crispin, but I let it go. "He's bursting with energy," I said. "He and Jasper might just wear each other out."

Jon lay half on his side, running the

fine sand through his fingers, frowning. Alone for about a minute since Crispin had removed Jasper, now they had me alongside. I picked myself up and walked up the beach to where I had left my towel on the rocks. Louise had disappeared. Only her air-bed was left behind. I stretched out on it, the hot fabric scalding on my skin, and stared up into the sky.

The weeks were wearing on. It wouldn't be too long now before the Summer School would be over and I'd be going home. Would Melanie come over to England straight away? Or would she wait for her divorce to be made final? I shut my mind on the possible next step. I had written my mother a cheerful, reassuring letter. Melanie was all right, I had told her. It certainly seemed that the Raoul affair was off but she wasn't about to do anything silly . . .

"Jon, *don't*!"

Melanie's cry was clear and loud. I sat bolt upright. Jon was at the sea's edge with his hands cupped round his mouth.

Melanie said, "He's too far out to hear you. And it might frighten Jasper."

I stared out into the bay. The air-bed had got to the entry to the cove. Jumping up, I ran down to where Jon and Melanie stood. "I do wish he'd come in." Melanie was holding down anxiety with difficulty. "I'm a hopeless swimmer. I'd never make it that far — "

"I'll go," I said and stepped into the water.

"No!" Jon's hand shot out and gripped my arm. "They'll be all right," he said, easing up. "In fact, he's turning now — "

What happened then I couldn't make out. Had currents caught them where the water surged in towards the cove? Or a gust of wind from the open sea? As Crispin put the air-bed round, it rose at one end with a horrifying slow deliberation, tipping Crispin and Jasper into the water. Paralysed with shock I stood unable to move. I was aware of Jon sprinting towards the arm of rock. He was up in seconds, leaping along the jagged rib. Crispin had moved fast too, and soon had Jasper out of the sea and on to the air-bed, a tiny figure dazzling with wet and sunlight. Crispin began towing him in. I relaxed.

"It's all right," I said. "He's got him safe. Crispin's a strong swimmer."

And then somehow incredibly Crispin had lost hold of the air-bed. I saw it go spinning in towards the cliff while he seemed not to be gaining in his attempt to reach it. I raced into the water. I am a reasonably good swimmer, I had had a rest. It would take me no time to reach the lilo. If only Jasper kept his head and held on tight! With the fast strokes I was doing I could see little, only the air-bed ahead, bouncing against the cliff and swinging off, carried out on long lazy waves.

Surely Crispin should have got to the air-bed by now! I trod water for a moment to check on what was happening. He was farther out than before, with a belt of broken water running between him and where the air-bed drifted. With horror as

I looked I saw him go under. He must be tiring! If I could reach the air-bed, could I tow it to Crispin to give him support? Sobbing, I lunged forward. The air-bed was only yards from me now. I could see Jasper. He was terrified, but not for himself. He was staring back out to sea. Crispin had surfaced again, briefly, and was going under once more. And as I stared, knowing it just wasn't possible for me to reach Crispin in time, I saw Jon Alexander jump from the cliff above, into the sea.

8

IT must have been an agonizing moment for Jasper, for in my dismay and despair I myself went under, dropping into those dark green depths, my senses spinning. But in seconds I was up again and in no time at all I had reached him. Words were beyond me. Choking, struggling for breath, I managed to give him some sort of reassuring sign as I searched for a good grip on the air-mattress.

Letting it take some of my weight while I fought to overcome deadening weariness, I scanned the sea ahead. A ridge of waves was riding towards me, on the point of curling and breaking into spray, and I could see nothing at all — no sign of Crispin, no sign of Jon. Why on earth, a non-swimmer, had Jon plunged into the sea? Had he seen a rock nearby that he had thought to

243

reach? Was it possible there was a boat out there beyond the point that he had signalled? He wasn't a fool. And then I saw a head and the flash of an arm. Jon or Crispin? Swimming or in trouble?

There was nothing for it but to strike out in the direction of the head I had glimpsed. The air-bed didn't hold me back. Although there is no tide in the Mediterranean it felt as though the sea were pulling me out towards the mouth of the cove. My ears roared, my eyes stung, my limbs ached. Jasper was clinging safely to the air-bed. I was heading for where I had last seen Jon or Crispin and that was all that mattered. When something hard struck me fiercely and suddenly on the thigh. I almost let go of the air-bed through shock. I didn't feel pain at all at first. That only came on a few minutes later in waves of sickness that left me dizzy and faint. Too faint and weak to swim — What on earth had happened to me? What could have struck me? Was someone down there with an aqua-lung harpooning exotic fish? It wasn't fair — I hadn't deserved this. I must be no distance at all from where I had seen that head and flashing arm. I ought to have been able to reach them. Crispin with the air-bed in sight could surely have put out a last effort — Jon, though he couldn't swim, must know how to float — I ought to have been able to save them. My hand clenched desperately on the flap of the air-bed as I felt myself going limp, my senses whirling, my body all searing pain. I mustn't let go of the air-bed . . .

What I was next conscious of was sky, pearly grey with sunshine blinding my eyes, jolting motion, my thigh constricted as though by some red-hot iron band. I struggled to free myself, I couldn't have told from what. From a long way off I heard voices, coming and going. Where was I? On a boat? And then sickening giddiness swamped me and I must have lost consciousness again. A nightmare sequence remains in my mind. Always there was light. There was movement, sometimes with the rush of hot air on my face. I was held in something rough that burned my skin. There was noise sometimes, a roaring in my ears. Sometime there was no sound at all, as though I weren't in a living world. Anxiety tore at me but I couldn't have said for what. No condition remained static. Conscious, almost through the fog for a few moments, I would go swinging down into an uncharted limbo of jumbled impressions and nameless terrors.

And then there is a blank of which I remember nothing at all, and at the end of it total consciousness, with freedom from sickness. I was lying in a bed in a dim, cool room, with only a single sheet over my body. I had a headache, there was a fierce beating pain in my thigh. I felt as though I had been badly beaten up. But it was all manageable and my mind was clear, frighteningly clear. Jon in the sea, and Crispin. Jasper clinging to that air-bed. *What had happened to them?*

A violent attempt to leap up brought the sickening giddiness back. I fell half out of bed and was caught in warm bare arms and eased gently back on to the pillows. Melanie's face swam into sight, smiling, her little teeth showing white under that short upper lip.

"It's all right, darling," she whispered. "Everything is all right."

I clutched her. "Jon — Crispin — Jasper — "

She laid her cheek against mine. It was cool. "All safe and sound. Nurse is going to give you something to help you sleep. No more talking now. You'll hear all about it when you wake up."

Of course I didn't. When I woke up it was very early in the morning and the nurse, who was French, and a gentle nun had come on duty long after I had been admitted to hospital and didn't know anything except that there was 'nothing to worry about'. I had to wait for hours, until the sun was streaming in tall windows and I had discovered that I was still in one piece with a bandage on an aching thigh, when at last Melanie arrived.

"Hi, there!" she said, perching on my bed so that I winced and she bounced off again and found herself a chair.

"What *happened*?" I demanded.

Melanie drew a long breath. "Well, you were going great guns, towing Jasper in the wrong direction until you went into a great jagged rock — "

"The wrong direction! I was trying to get to Crispin. He was drowning — "

"Not your glamour boy! He's too astute to drown! He had met a nasty patch of current after he'd lost his hold on the lilo and had the bright idea of swimming out to get round it and even going under it. All of which made Jon, too, think he was in difficulty — "

"But Jon can't swim."

"He found he could. He will tell you about that himself. He's outside in the car with Jasper. They won't allow Jasper into the hospital"

Jon — outside in the car! "Is he all right?"

"Pretty shaken. I don't think he'll fuss so much to go on the water for a bit."

I realized it was Jasper she was talking about, not Jon.

"Your Crispin will be along later to pay homage. A bit concerned about his throat — he swallowed rather a lot of salt water. He ought never to have taken the lilo out so far. How is your leg?"

"Aching."

"That rock certainly tore into your poor flesh and by the time Jon fished you out you had scarcely any blood left in you — " Jon had fished me out! Perhaps it was the mention of blood that set the room swaying.

Melanie said, "Steady on!" and held a glass of chilled orange to my lips. "Take it easy. I've talked too much. I'll be back this evening — "

She slipped away and I lay in the bed. Jon Alexander had saved my life! I closed my eyes. Any minute he would be in the room. What could I say to him? How could I face him, now, feeling about him as I did? I waited trembling. The sun had moved round and a broad shaft of sunlight lay along the floor. It was an aseptic room, high-ceilinged, white. The door opened and under the linen sheet I clenched my hands. A young nurse came in with an enormous bunch of glorious carnations.

"For you," she said. "I have brought a vase."

I watched her fill a vase from the wash-basin tap. Looking up into the mirror, she met my eyes. "Dr Alexander," she said, enunciating carefully, "asks me to say to you that he will come later. When you are no more tired."

I thanked her and smiled. I told myself I felt relieved. Which doesn't altogether make sense when I remember how the minute the little nurse closed the door behind her, I burst into tears.

Later in the day Crispin arrived, with a bigger bunch of even more glorious carnations. He set them down and bent over me to kiss me. I turned away my head.

His lips brushed my cheek. "Cross with me?"

"Why should I be cross with you?"

"Because I'm not a hero."

"Don't be tiresome," I said. "You aren't in an opera now!"

He sat down beside my bed. He looked tired and abject, which didn't suit him.

I said, "I got the most awful fright yesterday. Melanie has explained — You were trying to swim out beyond that nasty patch of current and come in so that you would catch Jasper and the lilo. From where I was, I thought you'd got cramp or something and were going under. So I complicated things by swimming out towards you. And then I saw Jon Alexander going in and I thought he couldn't swim"

Crispin reached for my hand. "Dear, darling Dinah!" Then he sighed. "I don't know why Jon Alexander made such a thing about not swimming.

And I don't know why he's doing this whitewashing job."

"What?"

"Well, you see, it wasn't really quite like that. That nephew of yours, my love, is a devil. It was his fault we went into the drink. He larked about on that air-bed. Otherwise it wouldn't have happened, even after I had got him back on board — and it isn't easy with a wet, wriggling fiend — he carried on his nonsense. 'It's my lilo! I won't let you get on!' I hadn't planned to get on. I was going to tow him in. Then, quite frankly, I lost my temper. I thought 'The hell with it!' and let him go!"

I stared at Crispin. *"You let him go!"*

"I sent him spinning in towards the cliff where I knew he couldn't come to any harm. And then I let myself drift out."

"You mean — when we all thought you were in difficulties — you were — "

"Giving that kid a lesson! All right, it doesn't sound so good now. It didn't occur to me that you'd all be watching and getting the wrong impression. Young Jasper *was* scared then! I had to laugh. I'm *sorry,* Dinah! That's the way it was. And then I saw you haring out and thought, 'Fine, Aunt Dinah going to take over!' I was getting pretty fed up by then. There were some rock pools deep down with weed and little fish and I took a few trips to have a look — But without goggles it's really no use — "

"When I was desperately trying to secure Jasper, praying that he would hold on to that air-bed till I got to him, you were amusing yourself sightseeing on the sea-bottom!"

His grin was shame-faced. "It never entered my head you'd think there was a problem. I saw you get to Jasper. He was pretty glad to have you there, I could tell that. I reckoned he wouldn't behave quite so badly next time anybody was mad enough to take him out on an air-bed! And then I couldn't believe my eyes. First, you start towing the lilo out to sea, and then Jon Alexander comes leaping off the cliff. It was then I realized. Jon came straight for me like a professional lifesaver. It took quite a bit of time to convince him I didn't need his services. He would have throttled me and held me under, only he was concerned about you and off he went. And, ye gods, this time he *was* needed! I doubt if I would have realized — not in time anyway. You got a dreadful gash on that rock. Dinah, I feel awful about this. I don't know what to say. Jon was marvellous, got you out, did a tourniquet, carried you to the car. Raoul and Louise had appeared on the scene by then. That was when he came out with his version of my daring deeds and fine intentions. I hadn't the heart to disillusion everybody. Anyway, we were all too worried. You kept passing out. But my Dinah, I couldn't keep the truth from you. You know me for what I am, a weak, selfish, frightened creature — "

"Shut up, Crispin!" With his last words he had been getting to look more solemn, almost noble, like the self-obsessed hero of a sentimental novel. "Of course you're weak and selfish and frightened! What human being isn't?"

I knew why Jon Alexander had put out the heroic version of what had happened. It was to protect me, to save my face. He believed I was emotionally involved with Crispin. Even if I got to know from Crispin what had really taken place, no one else need know. I needn't feel shame for my man.

"I'm tired now," I said. "Would you mind awfully if I asked you to go?"

"You're shocked. You're appalled at how I behaved!"

"No! It's funny, really!" Something flickered in his face. "Oh, I'll keep the joke to myself. You can trust me."

He went. I lay in the white aseptic room, laughed a little and cried a bit. The nurse when she came in said I didn't realize how weak I was. In the evening Melanie came alone and sat with me for only half an hour. "They said you were very tired and needed rest," she told me. And probably they were right, for by next morning I felt incomparably better. I was allowed to get up, I walked about. A doctor came who said I could leave hospital that day.

Melanie brought in my things. Outside, Jon Alexander had the car ready. Meeting him was an anticlimax. I had to heave myself into the car seat, make my farewells to the nurses.

At La Closerie I was thankful to find we had drawn up to a side entrance. There was to be no limping progress across the crowded courtyard. In the hall I leant weakly against a great stone column and struggled to keep down tears.

"I — I need a moment before all those stairs."

Jon said, "There's no question of your facing stairs. You're in a ground-floor room. Melanie knows the way."

It was small, dim after the white hospital room, with shelves on the walls holding a scatter of books and a barred window looking out on the garden where he and I had sat that never-to-be-forgotten evening. The bed was narrow and as hard as the hospital bed, but I was thankful to be 'home'. Melanie brought me my belongings from my room under the roof.

"I would have loved to have you with me," she said. "But it's quiet here, and you can get out into the garden."

The staff at La Closerie were old friends. The dimpling maid who had enjoyed Crispin's flowers before brought me the roses that arrived from him next morning, and when I felt ready, gave me an arm into the little private garden. I was lying in a chaise longue in the shade of the hibiscus hedge when Jon Alexander appeared with morning coffee on a tray.

"Don't sit up!" he said. "There's a table here." He set my coffee at my elbow. "All part of the service! How are you feeling?"

"Fine," I said and wished that I was.

"You're looking peaky still."

"Thanks!"

He laughed.

I sipped the hot strong coffee and gathered my forces.

"I have to thank you," I said. "For saving my life."

His face tautened. "Forget all about it!"

"I can hardly forget all about it — "

"I suppose not." He set down his cup. "If it hadn't been for a hang-up of my own — Oh, never mind! Let's leave it, shall we? All your friends keep asking for you. Mrs Benson particularly asked me to say — "

"By hang-up, you mean your saying you didn't swim?"

He had lifted up his cup. Now he set it down again.

"If you hadn't believed I couldn't swim you wouldn't have gone out after Crispin. You'd have known you could leave him to me. And, in any case, he wasn't in need of either of us."

"He has told me — all of it."

Jon was staring hard at the short spiky grass that passes for lawn in the garden at La Closerie. "He didn't have to. Giving Jasper a lesson — Well, he has a bit to learn about child psychology. But any fault there was, was mine."

"No!"

He got up, his coffee forgotten. "Please don't brood about it. It's a long way in the past. It's just that I did once allow someone to die — from drowning. She was rather like you, actually. To look at — not in herself. I think maybe that's why — since we are talking about it — that first day you came to see me at Bexton about the job — Your hair was wet. It was like seeing a ghost. I didn't want to be reminded — to face up to what I'd been trying to hide from. I panicked, I think. Can you understand? That's why I was rude. Anyway I didn't ever swim again. I wish I needn't have said any of this. But I realize I do owe you some explanation. Please — please don't think about it and let it upset you. Now I must go, I've got a class."

He strode away between the oleanders.

"Jon!" I cried, struggling to get up. "Come back!" But he disappeared round the lichened buttress of the old monastic building.

I sank back in my chair, my heart aching for him. So that was it, the root of his bleakness and loneliness! Through some lack of care on his part someone had died, and he hadn't been able to forgive himself, to come to terms with it. A girl — *like me!* Had he cared for her? Or was it that he had felt responsible? And in these last weeks — after how long I had no means of knowing — he had been coming to acceptance, a readiness to live again. I had been aware of a change in him since we had been in St Pierre-de-Lys. I had seen him become easier, relaxed, he had looked younger, happier. Because he had met my sister. He had been brought back to life by her out-going warmth. And I had grudged it to him.

Melanie found me lying limp in my chair, my eyes closed. "This proving too much for you, darling?" She was in white slacks today, with a clinging black top and rows of gold chains. There was an air of suppressed excitement about her.

I said, "No. I'm fine."

She sat down on the grass. "You haven't finished your coffee."

"Jon brought it. He told me why he'd had a block about swimming."

"Ah." The sound of the traffic came muted from the street, emphasizing the garden's quiet. "He terribly didn't want to. I said he must. How much did he tell you?"

"That someone died from drowning — because of him."

"His wife."

"*What did you say?*" I came bolt upright in my chair, staring at Melanie in dismay.

"It was years ago. He was in his first job — assistant lecturer at some university, I forget which. They came

261

out to France somewhere in the Alps for a holiday, their first since they'd been married. Most of the time they went walking, but they did some swimming too. She was terrified of going out of her depth. A young man in the hotel — 'a yob with beads and hair' Jon says — It was some years back, remember — kept making up to her and she doesn't seem to have had the wit to hold him off. Maybe she was flattered by the attention! The yob teased her, persuaded her to go farther out in the lake with him. Jon tried to protect her but maybe she had to prove something to somebody — or to herself. Anyway, Jon got angry. He was jealous. He left them to it and took himself off for a walk. It happened while he was on the mountain. Heart failure. These lakes in the Alps are deep and glacier cold."

I had my face in my hands. I hadn't ever imagined anything like this.

"Of course it was absolutely not his fault. But he feels if he hadn't got steamed up he would have been on the spot. He might have been in time to save her. It damaged him, froze him. Not swimming again was the least of it. He was consumed with guilt — afraid ever since of making relationships, of getting close to people. He threw up his job and spent months in some kind of community service. Then he got into Extra-Mural, dealing with older people as you know, often people who have missed out. He's made it his whole life. But he's beginning to emerge. The wound is healing. He says so himself. He's going to be all right."

Oh, Jon! Anything in the world, if you might be all right!

Melanie squeezed my hand. "Don't fret about it, Dinah. Life is full of cruelties."

Yes, life was full of cruelties. "He said the girl was like me — to look at."

"He told me that too."

"Madame Romain in Paris — " I murmured. "What did she mean, I wonder?"

"Who?"

263

I explained about that *jolie laide.* It was easier than trying to speak about Jon. Melanie smiled. "She must have seen the resemblance too. She must have wished it otherwise."

Dark hair, eyes like midnight — it wouldn't have made any difference.

Melanie said, "I'll help you back to your room. I've had to tell all the students not to send you flowers. You would have been smothered in them!" She got me out of the chair. "I haven't been able to stop Crispin, of course. Those roses today! And he has suggested dropping in tonight to give you a private recital, as you aren't going to be fit to get to the Final."

I paused on the flagstones by the side door. "Aren't I?"

"To sit on a hard chair while four competitors do their stuff? And then all the hoohah! No way! We shan't have privileged seats this time. I've had an up-and-downer with Raoul."

"Melanie, *no!* Because of my stupid

accident and all the trouble I gave him?"

"Nothing to do with you, my love!" she said airily. "He had some idea that if he hung around and was nice to my little sister and my friends I would turn back to him in the end. But I've seen sense in time and he doesn't like it!"

I spent the afternoon when I wasn't brooding about Jon reading in that dim cool room. Among a selection of standard French texts I found, as though dropped behind, a volume of Browning's poetry with 'J. Alexander' on the flyleaf. So this had been his room and he had moved out to save me coping with the stairs! Was there no end to the extent of his unobtrusive care for other people?

In the evening Crispin came and gave his private recital. The only room with a piano was stuffy and dark and the piano was out of tune. Crispin took everything with great good-nature, playing his own accompaniment as best he could. He sang the glorious love aria from *La Traviata* where Alfredo declares his passion for Violetta, gazing steadfastly at me as he did so, then a group of songs that the composer Haydn put to music when he was on a visit to London in 1794.

> *"My heart, secure in its treasure,*
> *Is blest beyond measure"*

His voice was radiant, his face glowing. When he finished we clapped like mad, Melanie, Jon and I, certain that he would carry off the prize at the Final in a couple of days' time. We had drinks after that in Jon's office and wandered out into the gardens at the side. The sky was dark with great flashing stars. A breeze sighed among the trees. Crispin led me away from the light cast by the windows of La Closerie and kissed me in the shadow of a cypress hedge.

"Think of me, won't you?" he whispered. "Will me to sing well!"

"St Cecilia will look after you. You

will sing beautifully — "

"Beautifully isn't enough — "

"All right, then. You will sing with everything just as the adjudicators would want it!"

He let me go. He was restless again, not in the mood for love and I was glad of that. We made our way back over the grass. Ahead of us Melanie and Jon weren't aware we were so near. I heard Jon say, "I think it's time you told Dinah. I was going to sound her out but I never had a chance. Surely she will be pleased?"

Melanie gave her snorting laugh. "I don't care whether she's pleased or not. Or anybody else, for that matter. It's us I care about!"

Back indoors they all said how pale I looked and that I had been overdoing it and must get off to bed.

I returned to the life of La Closerie the next day and the day after that I insisted on going back to my little office. I had expected Jon Alexander would bundle me out, but it was almost as if he understood that I had at all costs to have something to occupy my mind. By late afternoon I was weak with exhaustion and I didn't argue when he said, "Enough!"

He walked with me along the flagged corridor to what had been his room. At the door he said, "Try not to worry tonight! Even if he doesn't win, he's got what it takes!"

So that was why he had been so gentle and considerate! He had imagined I was worrying about Crispin and the Final.

He and Melanie came to see me at the end of the evening. Crispin had sung gloriously, the applause had been rapturous. But the judges had placed him second to the French mezzo-soprano.

"The *mezzo?*" I stared at Melanie and Jon. It went to show how little I really knew or understood of music or singing. I hadn't even thought her good! Jon slipped out with heavy tact. Melanie said, "Not to worry! Raoul is taking him under his wing and Raoul does know what he's about. He has fixed an interview for him with this man he knows and Crispin is off to Paris tomorrow."

She moved to the window where she stood just beyond the light from the reading-lamp. In a dress of dark crimson, with her rich golden hair falling on her shoulders she looked as lovely as I had ever seen her. There was a bloom about her, a deep serenity that spoke of happiness. She turned as though from some dream and said, "Now sleep well and take it easy during the day. I'm cooking a nice dinner tomorrow evening and Jon will bring you."

So they were going to give me their news together!

Next morning I worried about whether or not to contact Crispin. As hopeful of winning the competition as he had been, he could well prefer silence from his friends. Before I had decided what to do, I received a note from him.

No roses, no card! "By the time you get this, Cecilia and I will have left for Paris, in our search for fame and fortune. You were lovely to know. Maybe, some day, who knows — we may meet again! Meantime, my thanks. *Au revoir.* Crispin."

I knocked off early to rest before what I knew would be a difficult evening. I washed my hair, I put on a bright pretty dress. Jon walked me to the car and fussed over me as he settled me in.

"I'm all right, really."

"It's an ugly gash under that dressing," he said. "I know!"

They had obviously planned this as a diversion for me after being shut up so long and now bereft of Crispin.

Jasper met us by the fountain as I made my way painfully over the cobbles from where we had had to leave the car. He was dressed up with his absurd bowtie and was in high excitement. It was the first time I'd seen him since our adventure in the sea and in spite of what Melanie had said, he looked as though it might never have happened. The *atelier* was dark after the brilliant sunshine outside. Instinctively I bent my head as I stepped under the lintel.

Melanie met me just inside. She was in a loose kaftan, her hair drifting over her face. "It's lovely to see you here again, darling!" she cried and flung her arms round me and hugged me hard. She was breathless and trembling. I braced myself. *Let it be now,* I thought. *Let's get it all said!* And then over her shoulder I saw Daniel. In a dark shirt and dark slacks with his great dark head, he had been merged in the shadows.

He came forward with his hands out. "Hello, sister!"

I stared into those dark smiling velvet eyes.

Melanie's arm was still round me. She said, "Dinah, say you're happy for us!"

Taken so completely off-balance I was frozen. I tried to speak but my lips wouldn't move.

"Oh dear," said Daniel. "We were

271

rather hoping you would prove an ally, an ambassadress who would carry reassuring despatches for us across the Channel!"

"Dinah has been ill." Jon spoke sharply. "I did suggest — "

Melanie drew her arm from my waist. " — that we should break the terrible news to Dinah gently." She moved over to Daniel and stood beside him. Jasper charged in from the kitchen and wedged himself between them. "Well, Dinah, it's just too bad if they don't like it at home. But Daniel and I are staying together."

I can't remember exactly what happened then. I rather think I began to cry. I was still weak, after all, and I had been waiting for very different news.

"I'm — *thrilled* for you!" I sniffed. "Really thrilled! So terribly happy! You've no idea!"

Tartly Melanie said, "You certainly sound happy!" Jon got me into a chair. Daniel put a glass in my hand. He bent his dark head close. "You and I were always friends."

"*Of course!* And they will be pleased at home. Of course they will!" I thought of my mother, how she had come to like Daniel, how she had tried hard to bring him and my father together only to have everything blow up in her face when Daniel walked out on Melanie. "But why didn't you *tell* me?"

Melanie snorted. "Didn't you notice?"

"Of course I noticed. Quite a lot. But I thought — "

"Yes?"

We stared at each other, she and I. I had said too much. "What did you think?" There was a dangerous edge to her voice. I saw a shadow on Daniel's face. He must have been bitterly jealous of Raoul. And she had been consistent about Raoul. She hadn't been dithering, looking over her shoulder to him, and the security he offered. I had seen signs but I had misread them entirely.

"I knew you were happy," I said. "I had no idea you had been seeing Daniel. I thought — "

"Well? You thought?"

I glanced at Jon. He looked blank, startled and then suddenly he reddened.

Melanie drew a long breath. "*Jon!* Jon has been a dear friend," she said. "He helped me to trust my own instincts, face up to all sorts of truths!" She knelt beside me in my chair. "You really are a prize goose! You and I will have to have a girls' talk later. Come along now. You're obviously in need of sustenance and there's a good dinner spoiling."

It proved to be a good dinner. Daniel acted as host as if he had never left the *atelier*. They talked at once, Melanie and Daniel, about his peace-offering with the picture, the significance of Melanie's unwillingness to sell it, their realization that being apart or with anybody else just wasn't any good. They weren't dewy-eyed. They would quarrel. Daniel might walk out again, but if he did both would know that he would be back. My visit to his show had played its part. It was through what I had said that he knew Melanie had not sold the picture.

In due course Daniel put his son to bed. Jon and I left early.

Arrived at La Closerie, he said, "What about a lager?"

"I'd love a lager."

He helped me into the little side garden. "I'm *sorry*," I said, when he joined me with the drinks. "What you must think of me I shudder to imagine! It was just that you and Melanie were together so much, you seemed so close — "

"We were. We both needed someone to talk to. I realized she still wanted Daniel. From one or two things she told me I guessed he was just waiting for a chance to come back — without losing face. He had really believed she was going to marry Raoul."

"We all believed that."

"But when it came to the pinch she couldn't. Her instincts were right. That wouldn't have worked."

"Do you imagine *this* will work, Melanie and Daniel staying together?"

"Yes."

"You sound very sure."

"They shared real happiness. Since they split up they've both been through it. They really know now what they value in life. If only your parents could be warm about it!"

"Mother will be. Dad too, once he's had time to think. He hated the way they started off. But once they were married and they had Jasper he hated the idea of a divorce."

From the courtyard I could hear the voices of the students faint above the muted sound of the traffic.

"I'm sorry you had it sprung on you like that. I did want to talk to you about it before, but with one thing and another — "

"I know."

"Dinah." He leant back in his chair out of the light cast by the windows. "The Summer School is nearly over. You've done a super job and we're all grateful — "

Some of the evening's magic went. The minute I knew he didn't belong with Melanie my stupid heart had begun to hope. What a fool I was! Hadn't I seen often enough that he regarded me at best as merely a moderately useful member of his staff? That there had been times when he had found me a liability?

"I'm fit enough," I said.

"You're having pain still and you're tired."

"I'm *sorry* I've had these days off work — "

"Don't be touchy! It's not that. We've practically finished here. Anybody can wind it up. Go off to Paris! Have a holiday. See Crispin!"

"What?"

Jon's face was in shadow and I couldn't see his expression.

"He put a very brave face on it but he's bound to be feeling low."

He leaned forward. "Dinah, I know I've seemed unsympathetic sometimes — critical too. But I was wrong. I found out from other people what he chose not to tell me — about his teacher's husband and the bargain-buying and how Crispin put up with a lot out of loyalty to the teacher who had helped him. The loan he asked me for — he paid it back promptly. Not from his prize money. He'd organized money from his bank in England. He shouldn't have had to stand the racket. That old rogue Mellor ought to have let him claim his loss through insurance — "

Probably Jon didn't know all the story — about the girl at the beach café and the youths beating him up. But it was generous of him.

He said, "He is an able musician with a very fine voice. I know you are fretting about him — "

"*Fretting? About Crispin?*"

"*Aren't you?*"

"I'm sorry he didn't win the competition, although I gather that doesn't really matter much. He's terribly sensitive and he gets scared stiff at what he's plunging into. But he is tough as they come and single-minded. Crispin will take very good care of Crispin!"

Jon Alexander made a strangled sound.

I said, "You didn't have some sort of idea that I was in love with him, did you?" I knew he had thought so and in spite of everything was angry suddenly.

Surprisingly Jon Alexander was suddenly angry too.

"Of course I thought you were in love with him! Everybody thought so! Here at the School they were all sighing at the idyllic picture you made, the two of you! Melanie thought so! And if you must know, she didn't like the idea one bit! Getting involved with a musician with no security! What on earth were your parents going to say — "

"What!"

We were both on our feet, our voices raised.

"Melanie to worry about me! After what *she* put our parents through!"

"If I hadn't thought you were crazy about that exotic warbler with his viola da gamba and all those flowers in cellophane wrappings, don't you realize

I'd have tried taking you out myself — dancing with you, kissing you — D'you imagine I haven't wanted to!"

He had seized my shoulders in a grip that hurt. "Does the idea strike you as utterly absurd?"

I staggered back, jarring my injured leg.

"Dinah!" He folded me in his arms. There was support in his strength and an infinite tenderness. "Darling!" His face came down against mine. I felt the roughness of his cheek. His mouth close to my ear whispered words — Surely I was dreaming!

"I love you, Dinah. Just at first, seeing you brought back old things that hurt. And then I discovered that you were you, and the old things didn't hurt any more. I felt so sure you were meant to be mine. I thought if I could reach you, I'd be home — "

I lifted my face. His first kiss was so light that almost I didn't feel it. "I love you," I told him. "I've loved you for so long — "

But for how long I had loved him he didn't wait to hear just then, for he was kissing me again. And it seemed that this kiss was going on for ever —

THE END

Other titles in the
Linford Romance Library:

A YOUNG MAN'S FANCY
Nancy Bell

Six people get together for reasons of their own, and the result is one of misunderstanding, suspicion and mounting tension.

THE WISDOM OF LOVE
Janey Blair

Barbie meets Louis and receives flattering proposals, but her reawakened affection for Jonah develops into an overwhelming passion.

MIRAGE IN THE MOONLIGHT
Mandy Brown

En route to an island to be secretary to a multi-millionaire, Heather's stubborn loyalty to her former flatmate plunges her into a grim hazard.